When he went down to investigate, the trouble at the hotel seemed, at first, to be part of a movie. There was a motion-picture camera on the traffic island in the middle of Broadway, and there was a camera crew at work. A man who seemed to be directing said, "We're making some location shots for a picture called *Panic in Needle Park*. This thing at the hotel looks just right."

But there *was* trouble at the hotel. In fact, the lady in 8-A had been murdered during the night...

# Location Shots

# J.F. Burke

CHARTER
NEW YORK

A DIVISION OF CHARTER COMMUNICATIONS INC.
A GROSSET & DUNLAP COMPANY

**LOCATION SHOTS**
Copyright © 1974 by J.F. Burke.

All rights reserved. No part of this book may be reproduced in any form or by any means, except for the inclusion of brief quotations in a review, without permission in writing from the publisher.

All characters in this book are fictitious. Any resemblance to actual persons, living or dead, is purely coincidental.

A Charter Book published by arrangement with Harper & Row, Publishers, Inc.

This work is based on an original idea of Arthur Cooper.

First Charter Printing December 1980
Published simultaneously in Canada
Manufactured in the United States of America

2 4 6 8 0 9 7 5 3 1

*For*

*Rita and Ram*

# *Location Shots*

# 1

It was a balmy May morning in the bedroom of a luxurious apartment in the new forty-story Charmian Towers on New York City's old West Side, above 72nd Street, across Broadway and across Verdi Square from the once elegant Hotel Castlereagh.

Brown-skinned, bald, stockily built Sam Kelly, an amiable-looking man of forty-three, was being kissed awake by a thirtyish, voluptuous, curly-haired natural blonde well known to big spenders as Madam Bobbie. They were covered only by a sheet.

Police sirens wailed in the distance.

Under the sheet she eased one leg over him, then slid her body on top of his, and after a small adjustment or two she began moving her hips with a gently swinging motion. The police sirens crescendoed slowly, building to a fortissimo climax and suddenly dying with a scream of rubber tires on asphalt. Madam Bobbie collapsed gasping on Sam Kelly's chest.

He held her close for a long moment, breathing heavily and listening hard. More sirens, the ambulance's wild cry, voices of men shouting.

Gently rolling Bobbie's body off his, Sam reached for a robe that was draped over a chair by the bed and got up and strode to the windows. He opened the drapes a little. Bright sunlight shone on dark brown skin. He peered down into Broadway, fourteen floors below. Then he went quickly to the clothes closet and began to dress: black stretch socks, boxer shorts, white shirt with soft collar, dark brown Sulka necktie, suit and vest of light brown sharkskin with a thin blue pinstripe, black Florsheim brogues, and a small black Astra .25 "Cub" automatic in a belt clip on his right hip.

When he had finished dressing he put on a yellow straw boater with a bright gold band like a halo. It gave him an angelic look. He took his gold Hamilton railroad watch off the dresser and slipped it into a vest pocket. Its heavy gold chain looped across the vest to another pocket, ending at a heavy fob. The fob was a copper-jacketed .45 bullet. It had been distorted in shape by its impact when it was fired. Sam wore it as a good-luck charm. He claimed it had to be good luck because it had missed him.

Madam Bobbie watched him as he dressed. Her eyes were cobalt blue, large, and shaded by long, light brown lashes. Presently she spoke. Her voice had a silvery, singy sound, but the accent was Brooklyn.

"What's happening, Sam?"

"Trouble at the hotel," he said. "Street's full of cops. Squad cars and an ambulance. I wonder why nobody called me."

Sam Kelly's face was round, giving him a kind of cherubic look, but his features were fine. The mouth was generous but not thick, the eyes a soft brown like his skin. It was an amiable, easygoing face. The lower jaw was slightly undershot, giving him the look of a friendly bulldog. He stood a little over middle height, about five-ten, and he had the bearing of a man who is physically fit, though a bit heavy and no longer young. He walked with a slight, almost unnoticeable limp, but he was light on his feet and could really move if he had to.

His speech was clear, clipped, precise, Northern but not Harlem, though he had been born and raised around 129th Street and Lenox Avenue. He had class. His voice was a light baritone, graceful and powerful. It was his habit to speak softly, but the thunder was there.

Madam Bobbie got up, wrapped the sheet around herself, and went to the bedroom windows. Pulling the drapes a little apart, she looked down into Verdi Square.

Sam watched her, thinking how good life had been of late. He liked Madam Bobbie. She was gentle and considerate, and this made him thoughtful of her too, so thoughtful that in the year he had known her he had sometimes thought of marrying her. True, he had not spoken of it to her, but he *had* thought of it.

"They're just making a movie down there, Sam," she said. "Didn't you see the big camera? You don't have to go yet—unless you want to get into the movies."

"I see they're making a movie," Sam said, "but there's also trouble at the hotel. If those squad cars and the ambulance and all those cops were just part of a movie scene, I'd have known about it yesterday. It takes time to set up a scene like that."

He went into the parlor on his way to the hall door and stopped by a tall bamboo cage that housed a blue-black bird as big as a raven. It was a bird typical of the American tropics. In Mexico, especially in Veracruz, it is called the urraca and it is a kind of magpie. It will mimic anything it can hear.

This magpie's cage was delicately but strongly made, cylindrical with a rounded top, all put together by expert fingers, the kind of strong, graceful work done by the little Indians of southern Mexico.

The magpie eyed Sam, squawked, and said, very clearly, "Good morning, Sam!"

And Sam said, "Buenos días, Carlitos!"

The magpie mimicked him: "Buenos días, Carlitos!"

"Smart bird," Sam said.

"Smart bird! Smart bird!" said Carlitos.

Madam Bobbie had followed Sam into the parlor, still wearing her sheet.

"You know, Sam," she said, "you could move out of that lousy hotel. . . ."

"I know," Sam said.

He faced her, grinning, and took her chin in his hand, tilting her face up to his. He kissed her lightly. She was tall, about five-seven barefoot, a big mama. She was also a big madam, and her clients were likewise big. Sam was not one of them.

"Well," she insisted, "when are you going to move in with me?"

"Bobbie, baby," Sam said, "when you figure how a private detective can operate out of a callhouse madam's apartment and still keep his license, maybe I'll do it."

He kissed her again and went to the hall door, in no hurry to leave. She looked so lovable standing there wrapped in her sheet, he wanted to come back in and love her some more.

"We have a date for brunch," she said.

He took a cigar case out of an inner pocket, selected one and bit off a tiny piece of the tip, struck a match and let the phosphorus burn away, then touched the flame to the tobacco, pulling on it until he had a good coal glowing. Madam Bobbie watched him. He knew she appreciated the delicate aroma of pure Havana leaf.

"How about the Fleur de Lis?" he said.

"What time?"

"Around twelve?"

"Don't be late. I'm hungry already."

He kissed her lightly again, patted her fanny, and went out.

Carlitos cocked a golden eye after him and screeched.

2

When Sam stepped out of the elevator he was greeted by the doorman, a green-uniformed giant with the heavy brows and smashed nose of an old ring fighter. He even had the cauliflower ears. His name was Zebedee Watkins, and he was known as Zeb. He spoke in the Carolina accent called Gullah, but he had learned to control it enough to be understood by New Yorkers.

Sam returned Zebedee's good morning.

"They're making a movie out in the square since early this morning," the doorman said. "They started before sunup."

"That so?" Sam said. "Any idea what's happening over at the hotel?"

"Part of the movie, I guess, Mr. Kelly. You can't tell the actors from the regular characters that hang around." Zebedee pressed a wall button by the street door and it swung open. "Have a nice day, sir!"

When he hit the street Sam sorted out the situation at a glance. A motion-picture camera on a tall tripod stood on the traffic island in the middle of Broadway like an enormous bird, and at the moment it had its eye pointed toward the front of the Hotel Castlereagh. There was a police cordon in front of the building, and there were several squad cars, an ambulance, and at least a dozen uniformed cops. It looked to Sam as if there were more plainclothes cops than those in uniform. Then he noticed that the sign over Blimpie's on the corner had been covered by another sign: BURGER AND EGGS. And he recalled that only a couple of years ago this had been the name of the place, when Verdi Square was known as Needle Park, before the 20th Precinct cleaned out the junkies, driving them indoors.

He crossed to the traffic island where the camera crew was working and spoke to the man who seemed to be directing.

"What's happening?"

"We're making some location shots," the man said, "for a picture. It's called *Panic in Needle Park*. This thing at the hotel broke just right."

Sam thanked him and crossed the intersection. Broadway, Amsterdam Avenue, and 72nd Street came together here at Verdi Square. Looking north, you can see the time-and-temperature sign on the old Central Savings Bank high above the little park. Sam observed that it was 9:45 and 71 degrees. The trees in the park were in May leaf. A young boy was pedaling a unicycle down Broadway. Two girls wearing see-through blouses were coming out of the subway station. A pair of blond Afghan hounds were leading a fancy-hatted, tight-trousered Negro down Amsterdam Avenue. He saw the girls in the see-through blouses and waited for them. It made

Sam's gorge rise, and it reminded him of the only thing he objected to about Madam Bobbie: her profession.

Most of the 20th Precinct cops knew Sam Kelly, so he passed through the cordon with nods of recognition and entered the lobby of the old hotel, once known as the Waldorf Astoria of the West Side but for many years now a casbah for thieves, junkies, dope dealers, all kinds of whores, Puerto Ricans and blacks on welfare, Hindus and Pakistanis, horseplayers who had been happy bookies in the golden days of illegal off-track betting, and Little Old Ladies and Little Old Men who had somehow survived from the long ago when the money came down from West End Avenue and the meeting halls and banquet rooms danced and sang with weddings and bar mitzvahs. Then the Hotel Castlereagh had had elegant shops off the lobby, a sumptuous cocktail lounge, a fine kosher restaurant, where stood now not even a newsstand. A sign over the desk read: NO MONEY KEPT HERE AT NIGHT.

There were as many cops in the lobby as out on the street, though only about half wore the uniform. The other half, plainclothesmen, looked no more like the citizens of this hotel than cats look like canaries, despite the plainclothes. Sam had eyes that saw what they looked at and ears that listened to what they heard, and he quickly deduced that either there had been a murder or a big dope raid was in progress. And again he wondered why the desk had not called him, for he always left a number where he could be reached when he left the hotel.

A couple of young whores were coming in from the dawn patrol. He said good morning to them, and they smiled tiredly.

He nodded to a brace of transvestites, male, also coming in from their morning cruise. They simpered like Southern belles at his friendly greeting and all but curtsied in their eagerness to be grateful.

He nodded to a Homburg-hatted, Windsor-cravatted gentleman of the Curt Jurgens type. The gentleman carried a cane with a pistol grip. He bowed solemnly to Sam as he passed out of the lobby. An unemployed actor going to take his morning stroll, thought Sam. Or perhaps a writer. Or a singing teacher. The gentleman seemed to have cut himself shaving, for he wore a rather large strip of adhesive plaster on his left cheek. He also wore gloves. And Sam did not know him. A new guest, no doubt.

Finally, Sam smiled benignly upon the Little Old Ladies and Little Old Men who stood around the lobby shaking their old gray heads in profound disapproval of the whole megillah. Few of them stayed on at the Hotel Castlereagh because they wished to. Most were living on fixed incomes, and inflation had caught up with and surpassed them. They were trapped, unable to get up enough money to move up to the Ansonia or buy into the Dakota. Sam considered them his special responsibility.

There was also a young and pretty woman who had the look of an actress, or maybe a dancer, about twenty-three years old, red-haired, green-eyed, with the classic profile of a Roman empress. She was Maria Devincenzi, known as Devvy, and she lived in the hotel. When she caught Sam's eye she crossed the lobby to him, elbowing her way through the throng of cops and hotel characters.

She took his arm and spoke in a stage whisper:

"I'm scared, Sam! Let me stay by you?"

Her voice was a sweet soprano, but it had a heavy, resonant undertone, and the low tones came through strongly. She sounded like what she said she was: scared. She also sounded like Brooklyn, tough and tender, dumb and smart, all at the same time, a New York breed. They do not grow them like that anywhere else.

Sam took her hand and patted it gently. "What is it, Devvy?"

"There's been a murder! A woman upstairs!"

"One of the girls?"

"No, an old woman."

"So why are you scared?"

"I'm just scared, Sam, that's all."

"Is somebody after you, Devvy?"

"God, I hate this hotel!"

"I asked you if somebody—"

"Is somebody after me? No."

"Not some freaky john?"

"I don't think so. I'm just scared."

"Then go to your room, honey. Lock your door. I'll look in on you later."

"Sam, what about the hallway? What about the elevator?"

"Devvy, with all these cops around, who's going to try anything? So go to your apartment. Or go over to Madam Bobbie's place."

"I wouldn't want to bother her. I'll go upstairs like you said. Promise you'll look in later!"

"Scout's honor. And be cool, Devvy. If you've got nothing to worry about . . . Is there something I should know?"

"No. Nothing. I'll be upstairs. Don't forget."

She began to move through the crowded lobby

toward the elevator, and he watched her as she went. If she weren't a hooker, he was thinking . . . On the other hand, he also thought, if you're sleeping with the madam, you don't mess around with her girls. That's the birth of the blues.

Because Madam Bobbie knew Sam could be trusted this way, she often recommended the Castlereagh to new girls. Sam would watch out for their welfare, and they were nearby if she needed them in a hurry, as when some client wanted to get up a quick party in her apartment for an important business connection.

Sam headed for the desk, shouldering through the crowd but careful not to jostle the Little Old Ladies and Little Old Men. He accidentally bumped into a hairy young threesome clad in long-fringed suede jackets, many ropes of beads, and ankhs—ancient Egyptian love symbols—shaped by a mischievous silversmith into tiny spoons for sniffing cocaine. Each of the trio carried a fag bag slung over the shoulder. What they toted in those bags was anybody's guess: grass, coke, speed, shmeck, uppies, downers, maybe even some acid. Sam apologized for bumping into them. Their eyes went wild, and they mumbled something. He moved on toward the desk.

A big, felt-hatted, serge-suited plainclothes cop was interrogating the desk clerk. The cop was a fat man about fifty, a stranger to Sam, who knew nearly every police officer in the 20th Precinct. This cop had the blue-eyed, square-jawed map of Dublin for a face, smallish eyes, heavy, dark jowls, thin lips, wide mouth, and a surprisingly high voice for such a big man.

The day clerk was Mr. Singh, known as Terry, a

Pakistani in his late twenties, thin, small-boned, dark as an African but very fine-featured. He was grinning at the cop's questions, but though Mr. Singh grinned broadly, showing a mouthful of ivory teeth, his forehead was beaded with sweat, and sweat glistened on his upper lip.

Sam said, "Good morning, Terry."

He was wondering why Terry Singh should sweat when a cop questioned him. It would have nothing to do with the murder of the old woman upstairs, whoever she was, Sam thought. Nevertheless, Terry Singh probably had something going for him, something like dealing a little hashish, enough to make him nervous around cops.

Mr. Singh said, "Good morning, Mr. Kelly. The lady in 8-A was murdered last night."

Sam said nothing immediately. He heard, all right, but in the presence of a cop he just naturally tended to clam up. He waited for Singh or someone to say more.

Besides Mr. Singh, the detective had been interrogating Mary Murphy, an aging chambermaid, gray and wrinkled, bent with a lifetime's fatigue. She was wringing her hands and moaning about having worked in the Castlereagh twenty-five years and never seen nothing like this. Life just wasn't worth living anymore. Sam patted her on the shoulder as if to say, "There, there, Mary! There'll be better days." But he did not say it, since he did not believe it himself. He felt sure that things were going to get worse. At the moment he would have made book on it.

Morris Feigl, the hotel manager, stood by the desk, apparently also being questioned by the big plainclothes cop. Feigl wore a blue silk Hong Kong suit and white patent-leather Italian shoes with two-inch heels that elevated him to something like five feet four inches. Aside from suit and shoes, his most distinguishing features were his tiny red eyes and his tight little mouth. His teeth were perfect, but then they were several years younger than their owner.

Sam said, "Good morning, Mr. Feigl. Why didn't someone call me?"

The little man grabbed his arm and said, "Come into my office, Mr. Kelly! I got to talk to you!"

"Just a minute!" the detective said to Sam. "Who might *you* be?"

Sam thought of a few side-splitters like Julius Caesar, Jehovah, Shirley Temple, but he did not think this was the kind of cop you made jokes with unless you knew him well.

So he said, "I'm the house detective, Officer."

He gave the cop his business card:

SAMUEL KELLY
*Private Investigator*
Hotel Castlereagh
2101 Broadway
New York, N.Y.          Trafalgar 7-2248

The cop said, "Kelly? *You're* Kelly?"

"Heard of me?" Sam said. "I haven't met *you* before."

"Private eye, huh?" The detective grunted. He sized Sam up, looking him over slowly. "Well," he said, "it's a first for me. In fact, it's *two* firsts."

"What is?" Sam asked, though he knew what was coming.

"Well," the detective said, "a black Kelly, for

one thing. And a black private eye, for another, a black Sam Spade. Hey, that's a good one! Wait'll I tell them at the house!"

"They know me at the precinct house," said Sam, as slowly and as coolly as he could. "But *you* seem to be new around here."

The big cop had been chuckling at his own joke. Now he stopped.

"Sorry," he said.

"It's all right," Sam said. "Happens all the time."

"No, it isn't all right. I want to apologize. Shake?"

"Sure."

They shook hands.

"Detective Lieutenant Michael Moynihan," the cop said. "Manhattan North. Homicide. Tell me, Sam, since you're the house dick, where were you when all this happened?"

"I don't know, Mike. When did it happen?"

"Well, last night, I guess. An assistant coroner's upstairs now. Where were you last night?"

Morris Feigl cut in, saying, "So he took the night off."

"Night off, eh?" said Moynihan. "Who stood in for you, Sam?"

"Nobody," Sam said. He turned again to the manager. "Mr. Feigl, why didn't someone call me?"

Morris Feigl hunched his shoulders, turned his palms outward, and said, "We should call you for every little noise? Last night it was just a little noise in 8-A like always."

"Not quite like always, Mr. Feigl," said Sam.

The woman in 8-A was registered as Anna

Jensen, and she was a friend of his own good friend David Christopher, who happened, just happened, to live in 9-A, directly above her.

"That lousy drunk!" Morris Feigl went on. "So crazy she talks to herself. Everybody knows. So she talks loud sometimes. Why should we call you every time she makes a noise? It could be nothing."

Lieutenant Moynihan said, "You call murder nothing?"

Sam was watching Morris Feigl closely now, thinking oddly of Hamlet's mother's comment on the Player Queen's protestations of innocence: "Methinks the lady doth protest too much!" Why should Feigl lie? Habit of a lifetime? More likely he had a little something going for himself, something like withholding the hotel-company funds, which would tend to make him nervous in the presence of cops. But Sam was certain Morris Feigl would have nothing to do with murder.

"What do you want from me?" the little man whined. "I'm telling you, we didn't know! She always makes noise at night, that lousy drunk!"

Mr. Singh said, his voice quavering with nervousness, "You see, gentlemen, it is like the fable of the boy who cried wolf. He was always crying wolf, this silly boy. But when the wolf really came, the villagers did not want to hear the boy, and so . . ."

Lieutenant Moynihan said, "And where were *you* when the lady in 8-A cried wolf last night?"

"Oh, sir, I only work daytimes," Mr. Singh said, smiling.

Sam glanced at 8-A's mailbox. There was a letter. He wondered about her telephone call slips. He could hardly ask Terry Singh for them now, with this cop standing by.

## LOCATION SHOTS

An elevator door opened and three ambulance attendants brought a body on a stretcher through the throng of cops and citizens of the hotel and set it down by Lieutenant Moynihan. It was covered with a sheet.

Without asking the detective's leave, Sam reached down and pulled the sheet aside, revealing the corpse of a woman in late middle age, the face battered and bloody, the throat neatly cut. He covered her face.

"Beaten to death," he said.

"You didn't notice, Sam," said Lieutenant Moynihan. "Her throat's been cut."

"*You* didn't notice, Mike. The cut on her throat hasn't bled."

Another elevator door opened and a smartly dressed Chinese carrying a small black bag made his way through the crowd to the desk. He spoke to Lieutenant Moynihan in an accent broadly British. Except for his mongoloid face, he could have passed, from the fine brogues on his feet and the handsome Savile-tailored suit to the elegant cravat. His hat was a jaunty fedora. His manner was correct, genteel, almost but not quite friendly. Most New Yorkers would have called him cool. Sam thought him uppity and liked him for it.

He said, "I have already reported my findings to Detective Commander Fuseli. I expect to have—"

"Fuseli!" said Sam. "Here?"

"I beg your pardon?" said the Chinese.

"Sorry," Sam said. "Please go on."

"My full report should be ready late this afternoon," the Chinese gentleman said. "Meanwhile it appears that this woman died from a beating she received, not from the cut in her throat. The carotid artery was severed by a very sharp instrument, possibly a scalpel or a straight razor, not an ordinary knife, but she was already dead when her throat was cut. She was beaten by rather large fists, I should add, almost certainly a man's. I shouldn't be surprised if her skull was fractured. At any rate, it was the beating that killed her. The throat was cut as an afterthought, you might almost say, perhaps to make assurance doubly sure."

Sam said, "Or perhaps her throat was cut by a second person? He—or she—could see that the woman had been beaten, of course, but might not know she was dead. She might have appeared to be merely unconscious."

"An interesting observation," the Chinese gentleman said, bowing slightly. He offered his hand. "May I have the pleasure, sir? I am Dr. James Wu, Assistant Coroner."

"Sam Kelly, hotel detective and private investigator," Sam said, taking Dr. Wu's hand. "I'm pleased to know you, Dr. Wu."

"How about the time of death, Wu?" asked Lieutenant Moynihan.

"About six hours ago," Dr. Wu said.

"That would make it around four this morning," Moynihan said. "She was beaten to death at four A.M., and her throat was cut afterwards. How long afterwards, Wu?"

"I doubt that we could determine the time," Dr. Wu said. "Of course, you detectives may turn up something non-medical that would help you there. Good luck! Call my office at five this afternoon, Lieutenant, and we should have everything for you." He paused and looked from Moynihan to

Sam, bowed slightly, and said, "Good day, gentlemen."

Sam watched the dapper little Chinese as he made his way deftly through the crowded lobby, followed by the ambulance attendants and their grisly burden.

"I'd like to have a look at the apartment," he said to Moynihan. "Maybe I could be of some help. I knew Anna Jensen slightly. I might notice something."

"Good idea," Moynihan said. "The Detective Commander will want to ask you some questions anyway. I take it you know Commander Fuseli."

"Indeed I do," Sam said.

Morris Feigl, who had been standing nervously to one side, put a hand on Sam's arm and said, "Before you go, I would like a private word with you, Mr. Kelly."

Sam moved a few steps away from the desk, far enough so Lieutenant Moynihan could not hear, and leaned down so Feigl could speak in his ear.

"We called you last night, Mr. Kelly," the little man said. "There was no answer at the number you left. I didn't want to say it in front of that cop. Who needs cops? The less they know, those shlemiels, the better for everybody! Okay?"

"Okay, Mr. Feigl," said Sam. "And thanks."

# 3

When Sam and Lieutenant Moynihan came out of the elevator on the eighth floor they found Detective Commander Gerard Fuseli and some other plainclothesmen standing in the hallway outside apartment 8-A, which was located next to the elevators. They were smoking cigars and talking. The door of 8-A was open. A uniformed cop stood by it. Men could be heard inside.

Sam said, "Good morning, Commander."

And Detective Commander Fuseli said, "Morning, Kelly. Where were you when all this happened?"

"Shacked up, Commander," said Sam, keeping a straight face, not a hint of insolence.

Detective Commander Fuseli did not look like a cop, Sam was thinking. It takes more than a badge. He was tall, dark, and handsome in a way, with liquid brown eyes, a mouth made for ice-cream cones, lots of wavy brown hair, and a soft curve to his jaw. He was expensively dressed but not tastefully. He wore cravats with regimental stripes, though he had never belonged to any regiment. He held a Master of Arts in criminology from an Ivy League college. The N.Y.P.D. had sent him to school in a program intended to upgrade the general I.Q. of the department.

As Detective Lieutenant Moynihan had deduced, from Sam's remarks, Sam knew Detective Commander Fuseli. But that was a long story and one that Sam did not want to think about. He walked with a permanent limp because of Commander Fuseli. He remembered a fine young cop named Coogan, dead now because of this Fuseli, M.A. Crim. And he did not want to have to think of any of it.

"So you took the night off, Kelly?" said the D.C. "How are things uptown?"

"Swingy," Sam said. Uptown meant Harlem to Fuseli, of course, for where else do Negroes go when they want to party? Arrogance could get Fuseli killed before his time, thought Sam, and it was late already. "What happened here, Commander?" he asked. "A junkie rip-off?"

"A junkie rip-off?" the D.C. echoed. "Well, now, that's just what we're trying to find out." He had been chewing his cigar. Now he took it out of his mouth and pointed it at Sam. "Do you happen to know," he asked, "whether the Jensen woman had any money or jewelry?"

"Tenants of this hotel tend to be poor," Sam said. "But no, Commander, I don't really know."

"Some of your tenants handle rather large amounts of money, I believe."

"They're not my tenants, I just work here. Could

you tell me what kind of tenant handles large amounts of money, Commander?"

"Whorehouse madams and dope dealers."

"Anna Jensen was neither one of those."

"You know this, I assume?"

"No, I don't *know* it, Commander. I don't *believe* Anna Jensen was a dope dealer or anything else that handles a lot of money. She could have had a stash—money or jewelry, as you say. Many old recluses do, like the Colliers—"

"We know this, Kelly," the D.C. said. "We're not investigating the Collier brothers affair this morning." He fingered the knot in his necktie. "But never mind," he went on, "what I want to know is simply this: Did the Jensen woman have any friends or enemies in this hotel?"

"Neither that I know of," Sam said.

It was an instantaneous lie, and he silently congratulated himself on the instantaneity of his lying reflex. The dead woman had had a friend in the hotel, a close friend who was a close friend of Sam's, too—one David Christopher, author, white, age fifty-seven. He shared Anna Jensen's bottle from time to time, or she shared his, and on occasion they went out together to a neighborhood bar. But Sam was not going to turn Fuseli loose on his friend David.

He would look in on David later himself and see if he knew anything of the night's events. David Christopher was the only man Sam found interesting enough to drink steadily with, and when they drank together they did indeed drink steadily, talking and laughing all the way. David Christopher was the kind of author who has a fund of stories and tells them well, and Sam had a few of his own, so they enjoyed each other's company and had come to be known in the neighborhood as the Damon and Pythias of the local pubs.

"So!" Detective Commander Fuseli said. "No friends, no enemies. A recluse. But someone hated her enough to beat her to death and then cut her throat, unless it was a junkie rip-off, which I doubt. We found her purse open and no money in it, which might indicate robbery, but junkies don't beat their victims to death and then cut their throats." Fuseli shot his cuffs, displaying a pair of gold links as big as fifty-cent pieces, which they seemed at a glance to be: John F. Kennedy half-dollars, gold-plated. "No friends and no enemies in the hotel," he repeated. "Do you know if she had friends or enemies *anywhere* in the neighborhood? What about the bars? Did she hang out?"

"Good point, Commander," said Sam. Too close, he thought, too close. Even a dumb D.C. could get lucky. "It's a fact, she did hang out. She drank a lot, as is well known around the neighborhood, and of course she did make the bars."

"Did she bring men home with her?"

"Some."

"Any particular man, or was she particular?"

"No particular man. I'd have noticed if she had a steady."

"What sort of men did she pick up?"

"Lonely men, Commander."

"Cut the crap, Kelly! You know what I mean. What caliber of man did she pick up?"

"To tell the truth," said Sam, "I've never seen her in any bar but Donohue's, and Donohue's is a fuzz joint, so you can figure what caliber. Not bums, not hippies. Ordinary citizens, like off-duty cops."

Moynihan and the other plainclothesmen in the hall burst out laughing, but the D.C. did not see the joke.

"Are you trying to be smart, Kelly?"

"No, Commander. Just accurate. I shouldn't have said that Anna Jensen hung out. I've seen her in only one bar. You could get the wrong impression." Which was exactly what Sam wanted him to get. "You see," he went on, "Tweed's is hip, mod, swingy, whereas Mrs. J's Sacred Cow is square and pretentious, and Donohue's is different from both places, being a fuzz joint where the boys from the precinct come to unwind before going home to the wife and kids." Moynihan and the other detectives were listening and loving it. Fuseli's face was reddening with high blood pressure. "Donohue's is as safe as a squad room," Sam continued. "Anna Jensen couldn't have chosen a better drinking place. When she took a man home from Donohue's it was usually an off-duty cop."

Lieutenant Moynihan must have felt motivated to volunteer information, for he suddenly said, "She gave out a lot of free pussy, all right."

"That's interesting, Lieutenant," the D.C. said grimly. "Would you care to explain how you know this?"

"Oh, word gets around," Moynihan said. "You know, guys will talk, sir."

"*What* guys talk, Lieutenant?"

"I don't know, sir. When you're off duty you drop in for a short beer, like Kelly says, and you overhear things. . . ."

The D.C. turned his back on Moynihan and said

to Sam, "Let me ask you, Kelly. Do many Negroes drink at Donohue's? That is, besides yourself? I would imagine..."

"Not many, Commander," said Sam. He recalled now that the son of a bitch had always been like that. How would he like it if someone came on about Italians? You could hear him yelling for Joe Colombo. "No," Sam said, "hardly any Negroes drink at Donohue's. Sometimes I feel like an only child when I go in there. Now, you take Tweed's, on the other hand. Lots of Negroes go there, but they're not my type. Too hincty, if you know what—"

"Kelly! God damn it!"

"Yes, Commander?"

"I'm trying to conduct an investigation, Kelly. Just answer questions. Can you do that?"

"Sorry, Commander."

"Do you know if the Jensen woman ever brought one home with her? A Negro?"

"Not that I know of, Commander."

"Well, I didn't like the junkie theory anyway," the D.C. said.

Sam could have killed him. His head began to ache. He concentrated instantly on the thought of Detective Commander Gerard Fuseli dead with a .25 bullet where his heart should have been, and immediately he felt better. He listened to the D.C.'s next insult with calm amusement.

"I don't suppose she ever gave *you* any, ah—as the Lieutenant puts it—'free pussy'?" But seeing that Sam was not about to respond to this question, or perhaps even seeing that he had already answered it, the D.C. turned back to Lieutenant

Moynihan and asked, "Did you finish questioning the people downstairs?"

"Yes, sir," Moynihan said. "All except the night clerk."

"And what have you learned?"

Sooner or later someone, Sam was thinking, someone was going to knock this man on his ass. Or maybe do worse.

Moynihan said, "Well, Commander, it looks like we got a witness. There was a noise complaint around four o'clock this morning, the time of death, and the call came from right here, 8-E, across the hall from 8-A. The man in 8-E called the desk about a lot of noise coming from 8-A. His name is Saul Braun. I was unable to question him because he goes out early in the morning. He doesn't get back until after five. He's a cutter in the garment center, an old man, lives alone. The night clerk, Jay Murphy, took the complaint. Murphy's wife, Mary, is the chambermaid who found the body this morning. The Murphys live in the hotel."

Listening to Moynihan's recital of the known facts, Sam observed that the detective was doing the whole thing from memory. He did not have to refer to written notes. He was an experienced sleuth and needed no M.A. Crim. from an Ivy League college to recommend him. He had learned his stuff on the street, at the scene of the crime. If left alone, Sam felt, Moynihan could probably solve this one himself. But of course Detective Commander Fuseli would not leave him alone.

The D.C. said, "And have you questioned this night clerk, this Jay Murphy?"

"No, sir," Moynihan said. "His wife says he left

early this morning to visit their daughter in Brooklyn. I called out there, but the daughter's phone is out of order. Do you want him picked up, sir?"

"No. I'll take his testimony later. Leave word at the desk for him to call us when he returns. Same for this man Braun. Do you know what time Murphy left the hotel this morning?"

"Yes, sir. His wife says eight o'clock, before she discovered the body. That was at nine."

"I know what time *that* was, Lieutenant."

"Yes, sir."

"Did you learn anything else downstairs?"

Moynihan glanced at Sam. He rubbed his chin. He was thinking. He grunted. He shrugged his shoulders.

Finally, he said, "Well, maybe, Commander. It's probably nothing. The manager, Morris Feigl, says they did not call the house detective when the tenant in 8-E made his noise complaint. Feigl says they didn't call him because the woman in 8-A, the Jensen woman, often made noise at night when she was drinking. It seems she was a noisy drunk. According to Feigl, everybody in hearing distance complained about her sooner or later. He says he saw no reason to consider this occasion an emergency. Of course he was wrong about that, but . . ."

"I suppose, Lieutenant," said the D.C., "you have noticed that four A.M. is rather late for a hotel manager to be hanging around the desk?"

"Yes, sir. He says he just happened to be on hand because he couldn't sleep. He says he suffers from insomnia and sometimes gets up and goes for a walk around the neighborhood. He had just come downstairs when the noise complaint came through. He lives in the penthouse, on the seventeenth floor. He says he told Murphy, the night clerk, not to call Kelly."

The D.C. turned to Sam and said, "You were out last night, Kelly? I happen to know you were."

"I told you I was, Commander. Shacked up."

"Well, then, why should the manager tell the desk clerk *not* to call you, seeing that you weren't in anyway?"

"Commander, that's a good question," Sam said. Once again he congratulated himself on his lying reflex. Not an easy, flat-out lie this time, but a delicate evasion, a Little White Lie. And fast! The truth would have to come out, of course—his connection with Madam Bobbie. He sneaked a look at Lieutenant Moynihan. The big mick was watching him with narrowed eyes, obviously thinking. He would figure it out. Fuseli would not.

"A very good question," Sam said. "Maybe Mr. Feigl didn't know I was out last night when 8-E called about noise in 8-A. If Mr. Feigl wasn't in the lobby when I went out, how could he know I was out, right?" But he could see that the D.C. was not buying this line. All right, he thought, let's try the well-known watermelon grin. That usually gets it. He flashed about thirty-six teeth. "Maybe when Mr. Feigl told Jay Murphy not to bother calling me," he concluded, "Jay told him I wasn't in anyway, so why bother? That's more like it."

The D.C. said, "I don't think so."

"You don't, Commander?"

"No."

"Oh."

"You're covering up, Kelly. That's known as obstructing an officer in the performance of his duty, maybe even suppressing evidence, and when I find out what you're covering up, I'm going to charge you. The licensing board will pull your ticket. Think it over."

Sam said, "Believe me, Commander, if I had anything that might help find Anna Jensen's killer, I'd give it to the police."

"That had better be the truth."

"It is, Commander. And if you'll let me take a look around 8-A . . . You see, as house dick I've been in Anna Jensen's apartment a time or two, on some of these noise complaints, and I might notice something your men wouldn't."

"Kelly," the D.C. said, "I still want to know why the hotel manager told his night clerk not to call you if you were not in the hotel anyhow, and I mean to find out. But that can wait. So you go ahead, have a look around. Just don't interfere with the forensics men, and don't touch anything."

"Thanks, Commander."

# 4

Eight-A was a shambles—blood everywhere, on the walls, even on the potted plants. Their big, tropical leaves were splotched with blood. The splotches were dried now to any ugly brown.

A table had been knocked over, a chair broken, evidence that Anna Jensen had fought hard for her life. And the apartment had been thoroughly tossed. Desk and dresser drawers had been pulled out onto the floor and the contents scattered. The mattress had been dragged off the bed and the ticking slashed to ribbons. The slashes had neat edges, indicating that they had been made by a very sharp instrument.

A wastepaper basket wedged in a corner between the desk and the wall contained half a dozen empty sherry bottles. Bristol Cream. A nearly empty bottle lay on its side by the baseboard next to an overturned bridge lamp.

A tall bamboo cage stood in a corner by the windows. Sam had not known that Anna Jensen owned a Mexican magpie. The one in Madam Bobbie's apartment was the only urraca he had ever seen outside southern Mexico, where they are as common as pigeons. This one, however, did not stand up and screech and talk sass like Madam Bobbie's. It huddled, or cowered, on the bottom of its cage.

The cage itself had not been damaged in Anna Jensen's struggle with her killer. It was just about the only thing in the apartment that had not been overturned, unless of course it had been overturned and then set right again.

Sam wondered why David had not mentioned Anna Jensen's having acquired a magpie. Urracas are not all that common in this country. But then, it was possible that she had acquired the creature since the last time he had seen her, whenever that was. Decidedly, he would have to talk to David.

There had obviously been a hell of a lot of noise coming from this apartment during Anna Jensen's fight for life. Why hadn't David heard it? He lived directly overhead. Or had he heard it?

The forensics men were busily collecting the bits and pieces of Anna Jensen's life, cataloguing them, and stowing them away in brown paper envelopes: inexpensive costume jewelry—rings, bracelets, beads, brooches—and a pair of gold-rimmed eyeglasses with very thick lenses. The fingerprint men were dusting. A police photographer was shooting the prints. At the moment they were trying for prints on the nearly empty sherry bottle that lay next to the overturned bridge lamp. Sam kept out of their way and watched them work. He sat on a window sill. The windows, wide open, faced south toward Lincoln Center.

On this balmy May morning everyone had his

windows open, and everyone's radio or record player could be heard. Pachangas and mambos were dominant. Some of the tenants were singing along with their radios or record players, wild Carib cries, blood-curdling shrieks that could have been rage or terror were they not song. And then the sudden crash of a box of garbage, bottles, and cans flung out of a window to land on the perpetual trash heap that graced the ground floor on this side of the building.

The Hotel Castlereagh was built in the shape of the letter U, with the open part facing south. From the windows on the inside of the U came this unending stream of garbage. The crash of a box of trash and empty bottles landing in the middle of the night could drive a man out of bed and damn near through the ceiling, as Sam well knew. He had occupied an A apartment for several weeks before getting the one he had now, 14-E, on the north side, the street side. Of course there were always a few carefree citizens who would toss their garbage out the north windows, but they were rare and were usually caught in the act. Some innocent bystander would see them and report the deed, and Sam would come and throw their ass out of the hotel. But on the south side, the inside of the U, surveillance was impossible. If you lived on this side, it was either because you didn't have enough rent money or because you didn't give a damn. If you stayed drunk enough, the noise wouldn't bother you.

As Sam left the apartment he examined the hall door locks and the door frame. Entry had not been forced.

Detective Commander Fuseli and his plainclothesmen, Lieutenant Moynihan among them, were standing in the hall smoking and talking. Or rather, the D.C. was talking and his men were listening, or seemed to be. They were all smoking the same brand of cigar, apparently the D.C.'s brand, for he had several more sticking out of his handkerchief pocket. They were an expensive U.S. brand, and the smell of them made Sam want to get out one of his Havanas if only to kill the smell. He got his cigars from an old tobacconist in Spanish Harlem who had a source in Montreal. But he decided not to light one. Not that Fuseli would arrest him for possession of illegal cigars, but if he somehow recognized them for Havanas he might commandeer the stash. And Sam hated the thought of a pig like that smoking good tobacco. Let him smoke trash. Moynihan, however, you would be pleased to offer a good cigar. The big mick was not a bad sort. Crude, yes, but manly enough to apologize for that "black Sam Spade" crack.

Detective Commander Fuseli said with a smirk, "Well, Kelly, did you do any good?"

"I didn't find any answers," Sam said. "Only questions. Did your men come across Anna Jensen's keys? I didn't see them among her effects."

"Keys?" the D.C. said. "No, I don't think so. Do you make something of it?"

"No, Commander."

"Why would anyone steal her keys?"

"That's the question."

"I don't think so, Kelly. After all, whoever killed her was already in the apartment."

"And her eyeglasses, Commander?"

"What about them? Nobody stole *them*."

"Commander, she was so near-sighted she

couldn't see past the end of her nose without them. The eyeglasses were not damaged in her struggle with the killer."

"Come now, Kelly. Where does all this get us?"

"Do you know if the windows were open when the chambermaid found the body?"

"She says they were. You think the killer entered by the windows?"

"I'm just asking. Have you determined whether the apartment was tossed before or after she was killed?"

"Thanks for the questions, Kelly. When you get some answers, let us know. I can see you're a real private eye."

"You forget, Commander. I *am* a trained detective."

"I don't forget. I don't forget why you quit the department either."

"And why did I quit?"

"Because you're chicken, Kelly. Right?"

"I guess that's right, Commander. And speaking of chickens, someone has to care for that big black bird in the cage. I'd like to take it up to my apartment, unless it constitutes evidence of some kind."

The D.C. nodded agreement, smiling thinly, as if anything Sam Kelly wanted could not possibly be important.

"And the plants, too," Sam added. "They'll just die here unless someone takes care of them."

"Whatever my men leave, you can have."

"Thanks, Commander."

"That's all, Kelly."

Sam pressed the elevator button.

Lieutenant Moynihan asked the D.C. if he could go back to the lobby now and talk to the day clerk again. The D.C. told him to go ahead, and Moynihan stepped into the elevator with Sam.

When the door had closed, Sam pressed the lobby button, and Moynihan said, "Sam, you got balls! Lying to the D.C., and right in front of *me!* Why? Tell me why, Sam, or I take you back upstairs and feed you to Fuseli!"

"Would you care for a good cigar, Mike?" asked Sam, holding one out to him.

Moynihan took it, smelled it, and dropped the D.C.'s stogie on the floor of the elevator and ground it under his heel. He bit the tip off Sam's brand, tasting it with approval. Sam struck a match, held it away while the phosphorus burned clean, then lifted it for Moynihan to light up. The big Irishman puffed until he got a strong coal going. He took a long pull and inhaled deeply, and he sighed as he let the fragrant smoke drift out again.

"God in Heaven!" he murmured. "Where do you get *these?*" He took another long pull. "Holy Mary!" he whispered. "Havana!" He placed an affectionate hand on Sam's shoulder. "Boy, you've got to get me a box of these!"

"You called me *boy,*" Sam said. "Does that mean we're going steady?"

"Sorry," Moynihan said. "I didn't mean anything by it."

"Mike," said Sam, "these cigars go for one hundred dollars a box."

"Jesus!"

"Do you still want me to get you a box?"

"Christ, no! I'd quit smoking first. How do you handle it?"

"Enjoy the smoke, amigo."

"Maybe I better follow you around, Sam."

"You were asking what happened upstairs."

"That's right. What happened? Why did you lie to the D.C.?"

"Why? As for that, why didn't you tell him how you knew I was lying?"

"Hell, I didn't *know*, Sam. I just figured. You asked them at the desk why they didn't call you on that noise complaint last night. You also said you'd been out all night. So they must have known where to reach you, right? It figures. But you don't want the D.C. to know this. Why? You don't want him calling that number, right? Did you forget that *I* might call it?"

"No, Mike. You can get it from the desk if they still have it. You can call it or find out where it is and go there. Sooner or later you'll probably do one or the other. But I don't want the likes of Fuseli doing it. That's all."

"You really do know him, don't you?"

"So do you. All right, I'll tell you about last night. I spent it with a lady friend. And I don't see any reason for either you or the D.C. to go any further."

They had reached the lobby. Moynihan stepped out of the elevator. Sam held the door open.

"Where the hell are you going now?" Moynihan asked.

"To my apartment."

He stepped back into the elevator, and as the doors closed he saw the big fellow ambling heavily through the still crowded lobby toward the desk. He would be going after the mysterious phone number, no doubt.

As soon as he had let himself into his own apartment he went to his private phone, the outside line, and called Madam Bobbie. He told her what had been happening at the hotel, though not all of it. The question of urracas bothered him a little, but he said nothing about it. How could it be anything but a coincidence that she and the dead woman both owned urracas? Parrots, of course, even mynahs, but urracas? Coincidence, that's all. As for Morris Feigl and Jay Murphy trying to phone him last night on that noise complaint, he did not mention that either. Obviously Bobbie had unintentionally, perhaps accidentally, switched off the phone for the night.

"You know how cops are," he told her. "If they get your phone number from the hotel desk, they'll call you or maybe come to see you. So for the next hour just let your answering service handle the calls. I should be at your place by then."

"You said an hour?"

"Yes."

"I'll be ready."

He hung up. He thought he had better look in on his friend David Christopher now.

# 5

When Sam got out of the elevator on the ninth floor, next to apartment 9-A, his friend David Christopher's, he found one of the hotel's Little Old Ladies and a young junkie punk waiting. The punk, a skinny, pimply-faced white adolescent with stringy hair and droopy eyes, elbowed the Little Old Lady aside and got right into the elevator cage.

Sam reached in and grabbed him by the shirt front and jerked him out of the cage.

"Go ahead, Mrs. Wiseman," he told the Little Old Lady.

"Thank you, Mr. Kelly."

When the elevator door had closed, Sam shoved the punk up against the wall hard enough to jar his teeth. Then he cuffed him with the back of his hand.

"You get your ass out of this hotel," he said. "If I find you here tomorrow I'll personally throw you out. Now, git!"

"You can't put me out!" the punk said.

"Git!" Sam shoved him down the hall toward the fire stairs. "Any more back talk from you and I put you out today!"

The punk ducked down the fire stairs, and Sam rang the bell of 9-A. No answer. He rang again, then knocked. Still no answer. David could be sleeping off a drunk, he thought.

He looked up and down the hallway. It needed a cleaning badly. It always did, this place he called home, his castle. But the building was not all crummy. Some of the rooms and apartments were clean, like his own or Anna Jensen's or David Christopher's, or the Little Old Ladies' and Little Old Men's. Such suites had not changed tenants more than two or three times in twenty-five years and these were fine. The paint was not peeling, the carpets were not fraying, the kitchens had no cockroaches. But most apartments had housed too many tenants and had become human pigsties. What can you say of human pigs? They dirty the hallways and the elevators and the lobby just as they dirty the street, so that in the once elegant Hotel Castlereagh the street really begins at your apartment door, not at the downstairs sidewalk.

Well, he would go up to his own place and try phoning David. That ought to wake him up.

He took the elevator to the fourteenth floor. As he was about to let himself into his apartment, he smelled the pungent aroma of marijuana smoke. He crossed the hall to 14-A and sniffed the air close to the door.

He rang the bell.

"Open up!" he said. "It's the house detective!"

He heard two women's voices inside, hushed and

nervous, then feet moving around hurriedly, and the rushing noise of water as a toilet was flushed. That would be their stash going down the drain.

Someone opened the door on its chain and peered out. Sam saw only part of a face, a big, scared black eye, the soft curve of a brown cheek, one delicate ear, some bushy black hair. He had to look up to see all this. She was taller than tall. She could have stood up to the Harlem Globetrotters.

When she spoke there were magnolias in her voice, big ones.

"Yes? What is it, please?"

The air was heavy now with perfume, incense, and marijuana smoke.

Sam said softly, "If you can't keep the smoke out of the hallway, Mama, you'll have to leave the hotel."

"What smoke, Mister?"

"The marijuana smoke, Mama. And don't jive me!"

"Yes, sir."

"If I smell reefer outside your door again, you'd better have your bags packed because I won't give you time to pack them."

"Yes, sir. Thank you, Mister."

"Something else you need to know, Mama. You're lucky I got to you first. This building's full of cops."

"Mister?"

"What?"

The young woman unlatched the door chain and swung the door open all the way, revealing a very tall, very shapely body covered only by a sheer peignoir. She stood a good six-four, but she was built in proportion. Everything was big. She was pretty, too, and smiling now. It was a mouth men would die for.

"Come on in, Papa! Party's on us!"

"Who's us?"

"Me and my girl friend."

"Not now," Sam said. "Maybe later." He heard a sniffing sound. Either the big one's girl friend had an early summer cold or she had been snorting cocaine. But at least, he thought, you couldn't smell it in the hallway. "Watch the smoke like I told you," he said. "I don't care what you do in your apartment, but keep it inside. I live right across the hall from you. If I smell one whiff of pot smoke in the hallway, out you go flat-assed on the street."

"Yes, *sir!*" the big girl said. "Y'all come back soon! Hear?"

Sam thought maybe he would. He let himself into 14-E, his own apartment, aware that a pair of big beautiful brown eyes was watching him. He double-locked the door from the inside.

Then he phoned David Christopher's apartment. His friend did not answer. He told the day clerk to keep on ringing. Mr. Singh was operating the switchboard at the moment. The Castlereagh had regular telephone operators from nine A.M. to eleven P.M., but when they went out to lunch or to the ladies' room the desk clerk took over. The little Pakistani rang on. Still no answer.

Sam did some figuring. He asked Mr. Singh if there was any mail for 9-A. Yes, there was mail for David Christopher. Since the mail arrived at nine thirty, promptly, from the Ansonia substation just a few blocks down Broadway, either David had been out all night and had not come in yet or he had gone out this morning before the mail arrived. But David never got up before nine thirty. He could, of course, be very hung-over, enough to be still unconscious. A man of his age and heavy drinking habits ... Ambulances from Roosevelt and Knickerbocker hospitals wail up and down Broadway by day and by night, carrying hard-drinking men of fifty-seven years.

So Sam went down to the lobby and got a set of keys for 9-A. He also took the mail for 9-A and for 8-A, both David Christopher's and Anna Jensen's. He was a little surprised that Lieutenant Moynihan had not already picked up Anna Jensen's mail.

At the moment neither Morris Feigl nor Lieutenant Moynihan was in the lobby. Mr. Singh said that he did not know where they were. Sam asked him not to mention the mail to anyone. He told him he would turn Anna Jensen's letters over to the police, but he wanted to look at them first. The Pakistani grinned as if he knew what it was all about.

This morsel of conspiracy apparently jogged his memory, for he said, "Oh, Mr. Kelly, that big detective was asking for the telephone number you left last night—you know, the one you go to sometimes to stay all night?"

"Did you give it to him?"

"Oh, no, sir! I told him I didn't know the number and I couldn't find it. I tell them nothing, the police! I'm no fool!"

"Thanks, Terry."

"Any time, Mr. Kelly. You can count on me!"

Sam studied the street through the front windows. There were still a lot of cops hanging around outside, both uniformed and plainclothes, and the usual assortment of street characters except for pimps, whores, and junkies. These special citizens had disappeared, if not because of all the cops, then because of the movie crew, which was still working from the traffic island in the middle of Broadway, catching pickup shots of the action around the hotel. All the actors and actresses in the neighborhood, mainly from the big Hotel Ansonia and from the sidestreet brownstones, had the word by now, and they were profiling for the camera from every corner of the wide intersection, trying to get into the movies. Maybe some important producer would happen to spot them in the rushes. But the fancy-hatted, tight-trousered, faggoty pimps, and their junkie broads were gone from the scene, up to Harlem, down to Fourteenth Street, anywhere out of camera range.

Mr. Singh had come out from behind the desk and was standing back of Sam and a little to one side.

"Have there been any phone calls for David Christopher this morning?" Sam asked.

"No," said Mr. Singh. "I have been thinking, Mr. Kelly, how very strange it is that I should be so much darker than you and yet I am of the Caucasian race and you are not. It is strange, don't you think?"

"Well, I'm *half* white," said Sam. "My father was half Irish, and my mother was half French. But I agree, it's strange that you should be so black, Terry, when you're *all* white."

Mr. Singh went back behind his desk and said no more. He looked puzzled by the strangeness of it all.

Sam went back up to the ninth floor and let himself into 9-A. His friend was lying in bed, on his belly, uncovered, naked, a big man with a broad back, a thin knife stuck hilt-deep into the heavy muscle just below his left shoulder blade. A trickle of blood had run down his left ribs and dried. There was very little blood on the sheet under him. The knife must have reached the heart and stopped it instantly for so little blood to have flowed.

Sam stood by the bed, staring down at his dead friend, stunned as if he had suffered a blow to the head, and grief began to gather in his chest. He could only stand and stare. After a while he found that he was crying.

And he thought, Is it over, then? All over now for you, David? No more nights on the town with me? No more stories? No more women?

Then he broke down sobbing and fell to his knees by the bed. It was some time before he got himself under control again. When he did, he took a handkerchief out of his left hip pocket and wiped his tears away. He blew his nose. Grief turned to anger.

Whoever had killed David Christopher, whoever had hung that knife in his back, he, Sam Kelly, was going to put the son of a bitch out of business.

A strange, warbling, raucous cry came from under the bed.

"Baudelaire!" said Sam. "Come here!"

A big Siamese crawled out from under its master's bed, looking up at Sam and blinking.

Sam picked it up and cradled it in his arms. It spoke again: *Yeow!* And again Sam broke down weeping.

# 6

Well, the first thing to do, Sam thought, was to move Baudelaire up to 14-E. So he rummaged in David's closets until he found a cat carrier, and then he took the big Siamese upstairs. He made a second trip for the tinned food, the sand tray, and the bag of sand. Before he went downstairs again he made sure the cat was all right, food and water in bowls, sand in the tray. The big tom seemed distressed. He had gone straight to the bedroom and scurried at once under Sam's bed. And there he stayed, crouched on the carpet, eyes wide, nostrils quivering. Sam left him there. It would take the cat a while to get used to the new surroundings, not to mention recovering its normal feline composure after the shattering experience of living with a dead master.

Sam went back to David Christopher's apartment and began his hunt for the killer. The suite had been searched, thoroughly tossed, as in Anna Jensen's case. Desk and dresser drawers had been pulled out onto the floor and the contents scattered. Closets had been ransacked. If the same person had killed both David and the Jensen woman, he—or she—had probably been looking for something that David Christopher and Anna Jensen had in common, but Sam could not think what it might be. Aside from the drinking habit, that is. Both had been prodigious drinkers and had found each other late one night at Donohue's, where Anna was packing away the Bristol Cream and David Christopher was knocking back the Jack Daniel's. This had been going on for several months. There could be no question of jealousy as a motive, Sam considered, for Anna Jensen was a plain jane in late middle age and David's favorite young hookers had no complaint. He spent as much money on them as he had ever done.

Nor was this a junkie rip-off. Typewriter, tape recorder, stereo, and video had not been stolen. David's wallet lay on his desk. The wallet had been rifled, but if anything had been taken, it was not money. Sam counted thirty-seven dollars and change. David's wristwatch was also on the desk, an expensive Swiss calendar job.

He studied the body on the bed. The left hand was covered by a pillow. He lifted the pillow just enough to see the hand. The heavy rose-gold band with its big ruby was still on the third finger. Definitely, this was no junkie rip-off.

Then Sam saw the answer. At least he saw the *way* to the answer. There were no tape recordings visible. He searched the whole place and found none. And yet, Sam knew, his friend David had worked with tapes every day. He was of that rare breed of writers who almost never talk about their own work, least of all how they do it, and therefore not even Sam, his closest friend, knew much about it. However, during the several years of their friendship Sam had picked up a little. He knew, for instance, that David composed on the tape recorder and later transcribed on the typewriter, then cutting or adding where needed.

Not only were there no tapes in the apartment, there were no manuscripts—no typescripts and, in fact, not even any carbon paper. Sam knew that David Christopher always made at least one carbon copy.

A tape recorder with no tapes, a typewriter with no manuscripts. Ergo, the killer had taken them. Or, just possibly, the killer had *not* taken them because they were not there. David had stashed them somewhere. And wherever they were, Sam was convinced, they held all the answers.

There was nothing more he could do alone, at the moment, so he called the lobby and asked for Lieutenant Moynihan, and when the detective came on the line he told him there was another body in 9-A.

"Stay where you are," Moynihan said. "And don't touch anything. I'll be up right away."

David Christopher's apartment was one of the few in the Hotel Castlereagh that still possessed their original elegance, though it was situated on the south side, the noisy side of the building. The original tenant, a wealthy Jewish aesthete who had redecorated the suite in accordance with his own taste and considerable means, had lived his entire adult life in it. David was actually the second tenant.

As a rule, occupants of the better suites were keepers of pets and growers of tropical plants. They were also collectors of art works, mainly bad. Sam's friend David Christopher had many luxuriant tropical plants, particularly some elegant ferns, but, unlike his fellow citizens, he had a rather fine collection of objets d'art including a few pieces of ancient ceramic pornography from China. There were no paintings on the walls, only mirrors, large ones, for the A apartments at the Castlereagh were small. The mirrors gave the illusion of space. They served another purpose, too, Sam recalled as he waited for Lieutenant Moynihan. David had had a taste for young streetwalkers, such as may be picked up week nights in fair weather along Amsterdam Avenue and along Broadway above 72nd Street. They are pretty young things, and they will go for fifteen or twenty bucks a trick. They enjoy their work. They are amused by mirrors. Only you must be sure that the girl you pick up is not a junkie, for junkie broads are poison. They will rip you off if you let them. In any case, they are dull. David Christopher knew the difference.

Lieutenant Moynihan showed up with two uniformed cops and stationed them in the hallway outside 9-A. When he had looked the dead man over, and before he began to inspect the apartment, he asked Sam how he had happened to discover the corpse.

"David Christopher was a friend of mine," Sam explained, "my closest friend—in fact, my only close friend—so I often looked in on him. A man his age, fifty-seven, needs looking after, you know. Or maybe you don't. How old are you, Mike?"

"Fifty. And I know what you're saying."

"I'm forty-three," Sam said, "and I hope there'll

be somebody looking after me when I'm David's age. Or even sooner."

"I'd better call the D.C.," said Moynihan. "He and you really don't like each other much, do you? What's it all about?"

"I used to be on the force," said Sam. "He and I worked together. Narcotics."

"So you know him," Moynihan said. "All right, so do I. But I have to work with him. I'd appreciate it if you wouldn't make it unnecessarily difficult for me."

"I understand, Mike. I'll try to keep it in mind."

"Thanks," Moynihan said. "I think I'll just have a look around before I call him. Anything you can tell me?"

"You see what I see."

"Well, it's a nice place your friend had here. All these plants! The lady downstairs grew some too. And he liked art, I see. What did he do for a living?"

"David was a writer."

"Books?"

"Yes."

"Any of these?" Moynihan was looking through the bookcase. "He must have been a very smart guy, this David Christopher. I never heard of any of these books, but then I'm not much of a reader."

"He wrote the ones on the top shelf."

Moynihan looked them over.

"Children's books? Kids' books! You'd never think from the ones on the other shelves—science, history . . . Yeah. I see now. He read science and history and these others, and then he wrote the same thing for kids. I wish I'd had some of these for my own kids when they were growing up." He shoved his hat on the back of his head and clamped his jaws down hard on the cigar that Sam had given him. "Now, why," he said, "why would anyone kill a children's-book writer?"

"Well, I don't think it had anything to do with his being a children's-book writer," Sam said.

"No, I guess not," Moynihan said. "Why, then? How did he manage to pick up an enemy?"

"I didn't know he had one," Sam said. "I don't see how he could have had. He was a nice guy. Everybody liked David."

"Not everybody, Sam."

"Everybody who *knew* him."

"You're saying somebody who didn't know him killed him?"

"Or somebody who knew him only in the wrong way."

"You think your friend was into something you didn't know about? Or did you?"

"No, I didn't know he was into anything but writing children's books, drinking, and playing around with young hookers."

"What about the dead woman downstairs? Anna Jensen. This David Christopher knew her?"

"Some, yes."

"How much?"

"Well, they drank together from time to time, in her apartment or in his, or in one of the neighborhood bars."

"Donohue's?"

"Yes."

"Were they sleeping together?"

"I don't think so. He had this thing about young women. Anna Jensen must have been David's age.

I think they just had a drinking friendship. Or I *did* think so."

"Sam, the way I read it, they were into something together, and this got them both killed. So what was it?"

"I haven't the foggiest notion."

"Would you tell me if you knew?"

"Sure."

"Yeah. Sure. You lied to the D.C. when he asked you if Anna Jensen had any friends or enemies that you knew of. You knew at least one friend—David Christopher. Why did you cover up, Sam?"

"I wanted a chance to talk to him before you boys got around to it."

"You thought he might have had something to do with the Jensen killing?"

"No, but I thought he might know something."

"He knew something, all right." Moynihan prowled the room. "Someone was here with him last night—other than the killer, I mean."

Sam had observed the empty Jack Daniel's bottle on the window sill, the two water tumblers sitting by the empty quart, the lipstick on one of the glasses. The lipstick made a clear, strong print. It was a big mouth, whoever it was. He didn't believe it was Anna Jensen's.

"Why couldn't the killer have made that lip print?" he asked.

"Assuming that one killer did both murders," Moynihan said, "the killer has to be a man. The Jensen woman was beaten to death by someone with very large fists, according to Dr. Wu, so it has to be someone else who put the lipstick on that glass."

"Elementary, my dear Watson," said Sam.

"All right, Sherlock Holmes," said Moynihan, "how do *you* read it?"

"I don't," Sam said. "I just try to get at the facts. If I can get the right facts together, they'll tell their own story. For instance, did they ever find Anna Jensen's keys?"

"No," Moynihan said. He was looking curiously at Sam. "Have you been going over this place? Looking for keys, maybe?" He started the search without waiting for an answer. Sam said nothing. The big fellow might turn up the keys. He watched him going through David's things, the clothes in the closet, the kitchen and bathroom cabinets, the desk, the chest of drawers. No keys. Moynihan said, "It looks like we're getting something. I'd better call the D.C."

He phoned 8-A, the Jensen woman's apartment, and told Detective Commander Fuseli the house dick had discovered a dead body in 9-A.

Fuseli came running, followed by two of his plainclothesmen and a uniformed cop. He posted the harness bull in the hall outside the door.

"Kelly," he said, "what were *you* doing here?"

"Everybody has to be someplace, Commander," said Sam.

"You're too smart, Kelly!"

Sam said nothing. The D.C. proceeded with his investigation, asking all the easy questions and making all the obvious comments. Moynihan told him about Anna Jensen and David Christopher having been friends, according to Sam Kelly, and about the missing keys.

The D.C. said, "Kelly, why didn't *you* tell me? I asked you if the Jensen woman had any friends in this hotel, and you said no."

"Commander," said Sam, "I wasn't even thinking of David Christopher at the time."

God bless the lying reflex, he thought again, for without it a man could hardly reach the age of forty-three.

"I'm going to check you out, Kelly," the D.C. said. Suddenly he slapped his forehead and cried out, "The keys! Of course! That's it! Keys missing in the Jensen woman's apartment, keys missing here! Find the keys, you find the killer!"

Sam said, "Commander, about these plants, someone will have to take care of them...."

"Take them, Kelly, take them," the D.C. said. "Who cares?" He began to mutter about keys. Then he snapped his fingers at Moynihan. "Call Wu!" he told him. And when the Lieutenant had the Assistant Coroner on the wire, Fuseli took over. "We've got another stiff, Wu," he said. "A man this time. It looks like a double murder. Whoever killed the Jensen woman killed the man, too, so you'd better come yourself, since you're already on the case." When he had hung up he told Moynihan, "Go down to 8-A and tell the forensics men to come up here as soon as they're finished."

He might have phoned 8-A and told them himself, but neither Moynihan nor Sam was about to say so.

Sam said, "If they're through down there, Commander, I might as well go and get the bird and the plants and move them up to my place—unless you want me here for something?"

"I can't imagine what," the D.C. said.

Sam and Lieutenant Moynihan took the fire stairs down one flight to the eighth floor, and on the way Moynihan asked, "What do you make of it,

Sam? Level with me, now!"

"Similarities," Sam said. "That's all. Similarities."

"Well, whoever tossed the two apartments was looking for something," Moynihan said. "Keys, maybe?"

"Maybe."

"Your friend David Christopher and the Jensen woman knew each other, and they both knew a third person, apparently, who killed them both around four o'clock this morning. Or was it?"

"Was it what?"

"Were they both killed at the same time?"

"Or by the same person?"

"Keys," Moynihan said. "Much as I hate to admit it, Sam, the D.C. is right. The keys are the key."

But Sam was thinking of urracas.

# 7

In Anna Jensen's apartment the forensics men were still working. Lieutenant Moynihan told them Commander Fuseli wanted them up in 9-A as soon as they were through. There was another stiff upstairs. And did they need the bird or the plants? If not, the hotel detective had offered to take them.

The forensics men said they had no need of the plants or the bird. They had not been able to get any clear fingerprints off the bamboo cage or the flower pots.

Sam observed, however, that they had got some strong prints off the empty sherry bottles, particularly the Bristol Cream bottle that lay on its side by the overturned bridge lamp. This bottle showed two clear sets of prints, easy to read: one left hand, one right, and the two sets did not belong to each other, for the left hand was large and the right one small.

Lieutenant Moynihan phoned the desk and asked for a cop, and when he had an officer on the line he told him to bring two or three men with him and come to 8-A. When they arrived he instructed them to carry the bird cage and the potted plants up to Sam Kelly's apartment, 14-E. Sam led the way. After the men had set the cage and the pots where he told them, he thanked them and they left.

"Nice place you have here," Lieutenant Moynihan said. "You wouldn't think it, judging from the lobby."

He looked around, and Sam watched him. If Moynihan was looking around the place, he did it out of habit, like a bird dog quartering a field. He would have a look around if it was his own mother's house or the parish church. Besides, Sam was thinking, it was more than possible that the big mick had figured that the way to solve this case was to follow Sam Kelly.

"There's a quart of Jack Daniel's in the kitchen," he said. "Care for a taste?"

"Sure, if you're having one."

Sam shoved a tape of Chopin's études into the recorder, then went to the kitchen and brought out the bottle along with a pair of water tumblers and a tray of ice cubes. He set everything on the coffee table by the windows.

Madam Bobbie's fourteenth-floor apartment in the Charmian Towers could be seen directly across Verdi Square. At the moment she had just flung open the curtains of her bedroom windows and was coming out onto the balcony. She was wearing her bright blue quilted robe. Even at this distance, about a hundred yards, she looked bed-luscious.

The time-and-temperature sign high up on the Central Savings Bank just above Verdi Square read 11:00 and 73 degrees.

Madam Bobbie went back into her apartment.

Sam said, "Help yourself, Mike."

Moynihan dropped a couple of ice cubes into his glass and poured himself a modest shot.

"Very nice apartment," he said again. "Wall-to-wall carpeting, television, radio, record player, tape recorder, even a guitar. You play?"

"Some. Would you believe I sing folk songs? Spanish, French, Portuguese, German, Yiddish . . ."

"How come Yiddish?"

"I don't know. Maybe because it's easy. Some of my best friends . . ."

"Lots of books too," Moynihan observed. "You read a lot?"

"Quite a lot."

"So tell me, Sam, does a private eye read murder mysteries?"

"Not often. They don't tell it like it is."

"I don't read much," Moynihan said. "What's on the tape recorder?"

"Chopin études."

"How about singing a song?"

"Not now, Mike. I'd probably break up, what with David dead. Too soon . . . Some other time. But now you know the way, you'll come back and visit."

"I remember," Moynihan said, "I saw you once in Donohue's. You were drinking Jack Daniel's on the rocks. Bill waited on you. There was someone with you—a man."

"Probably David Christopher."

"It was about a week ago. In fact, it was last Friday around five thirty. I dropped in after work with some of the boys from the precinct."

"How long have you been in this bailiwick?"

"Just a few weeks. Transfer from the Bronx."

"Were you in Homicide up there?"

"Gambling."

"So why transfer? You had it made."

"The Knapp Commission. I guess the department decided to keep me honest. I'm lucky they didn't put me back in uniform."

"Well, you won't get rich in Homicide."

"I didn't get rich in Gambling either. I didn't join the force to get rich, Sam. All I want is to draw my pay and live long enough to retire to Florida. Maybe I'll set up a little private-eye business when I retire. How do *you* like it?"

"Fine. I'd like more of it."

"Slow?"

"What I get mostly is bodyguard and messenger work. Somebody needs a man with a gun and the license to carry it, I'm available. As for the private-eye end of it, I get a call from time to time, but it's almost always domestic cases—you know, divorce, adultery, dirty pictures—and I don't take that kind of work. If it's a legitimate case, the client usually ends up deciding he didn't need a private detective in the first place, when he sees *me*."

"The race thing?"

"You said it yourself, Mike. 'It's a *first*. In fact, it's *two* firsts.'"

"Sorry about that, Sam."

"Well, it's true, and most whites react that way. For some reason, they don't expect a black to have an Irish surname, and they don't expect a black to be a private eye. 'A *black* Sam *Spade*,' you said?"

"I could bite off my tongue, Sam."

"Maybe if I hung out my shingle in Harlem . . ."

"There you go."

"But I hate an all-black neighborhood as much as an all-white one. This West Side suits me just fine. We've got a heterogeneous population here, and I like it this way—Latins, blacks, whites, even Asiatics . . ."

"But your one-man private-detective agency nets you enough to live on? I mean, could *I* get by, with retirement pay?"

"You, Mike? Sure. You're white. You'd get the bodyguard and messenger work and the private-eye cases too. But I make out all right. My job as hotel dick here at the Castlereagh takes care of the rent. I just have to rustle up the beans and rice."

"You drink good liquor," Moynihan said, "like your friend downstairs. And you smoke the best cigars."

"My beans and rice are of the best also," Sam said. He opened the cigar box and pushed it across the coffee table. "Help yourself," he told Moynihan. They both took cigars and lit up. "What about yourself?" he asked. "Can you get by on a detective lieutenant's pay?"

"My wife works at Macy's. The kids are all grown up and gone. I retire next year. Ever been married?"

"In Berlin when I was nineteen. She died here in New York a few years ago."

"No kids?"

"None."

"I married young too," Moynihan said, "just before I went overseas in 'forty-two, an Irish girl from the Bronx. Five kids. Two dead in Vietnam.

Three daughters, all married. There's just the wife and I now, except when one of the girls and her husband comes over."

Sam said, "Mike, what are we going to do about Anna Jensen and my friend David Christopher?"

"I was hoping *you* could tell *me*."

"What about the missing keys?"

"I don't know what to make of that. Keys have got something to do with the case. I'd give odds on it. But what? Do you suppose the Jensen woman and your friend both had a key to something?"

"I don't think so," Sam said. "If each had a key to the same thing, say a trunk or a closet, then whoever stole the first set of keys wouldn't need to steal the second, would he? Yet both sets are missing."

"You wouldn't have any idea what kinds of keys your friend had on his key ring, would you? You must have seen his keys more than once."

"I don't remember noticing anything unusual. He had two keys to the hall door, like everybody here, and I remember one for a closet in the apartment. I think there were also a few small keys, but I don't believe I ever saw him use them. Maybe a typewriter-case key, or a key for his dispatch case..."

"Probably nothing there," Moynihan said. "How about the M.O. of the murders?"

Sam knew how cops are trained to think in terms of the M.O., the modus operandi. As a general rule, your criminal has a characteristic way of operating. Stranglers do not use guns, gunmen do not use knives, shiv artists do not use the strangling cord, and none of these are likely to beat their victims to death.

"Good point," Sam said. "It looks like two killers, maybe three. You've got a fatal beating, a throat cutting, and a back stabbing, three different M.O.'s. But I don't like it. I think the similarities are more significant: keys missing in both cases, both apartments tossed . . ."

"Well, it's too much for me," Moynihan said. "Let the D.C. worry. I'm going to lunch. How about coming along? We could kick it around over a hamburger and some beer."

Sam said, "I've got a luncheon date with a lady friend. But maybe I'll see you at Donohue's after five?"

"I'll try to make it," Moynihan said. "Thanks for the drinks and the cigars. You've spoiled me for cheap smokes. I owe you."

He left then, and Sam stripped and shaved and showered. When he was dressed again, he made sure he had Anna Jensen's and David Christopher's mail in an inside pocket of his jacket. He would steam the letters open when he got back from lunch. Meanwhile he didn't want to leave them in his apartment. The way things had been going, his place could be the next one to get tossed.

He switched off the tape of Chopin études and was just about to leave when the phone rang. It was not the house phone but his private outside line, so he took the call.

A man with a polite and pleasant manner and a heavy German accent answered his hello.

"Mr. Kelly?"

"Yes."

"I am calling you, Mr. Kelly," the man explained, "because I wish to engage your services as a private investigator. I have already put five hundred dollars cash in the mail as a retainer. You should have it by tomorrow morning at the latest. I have sent it by special delivery."

"Who are you?" Sam asked.

"My name is Richard Schmidt," the man said. "I hope you are available."

"What is it you want me to do for you, Mr. Schmidt?"

"Well, Mr. Kelly, a mutual friend has informed me that certain tape recordings and a typewritten manuscript—"

"Just a minute, Mr. Schmidt," said Sam. "Who is this mutual friend?"

"Anna Jensen."

"How do you happen to know her?"

"Does it matter, sir? She had the tapes and the manuscript, and I want them. I want you to get them for me. Will you do it?"

"Why do you think I *can?*"

"I am willing to pay you well, Mr. Kelly, very well indeed."

"Well, I guess that's a reason. What's on the tapes?"

"Do you need to know that, sir?"

"Not right now, I guess. What's the price?"

"If you recover those tape recordings and the typewritten manuscript for me, you can name your own price."

"Ten thousand dollars?"

"Certainly. Ten thousand."

"Fifty thousand?"

"Even fifty thousand."

"A hundred thousand?"

"Come, Mr. Kelly, are you negotiating with me already? Perhaps you know where the tapes and the manuscript are?"

"Perhaps. How can I get in touch with you?"

"*I* will get in touch with *you*, sir. Do you know

where the tapes and manuscript are?"

"Call me at ten o'clock sharp tomorrow morning. Your retainer should be here by then."

"Then you do know something about the tapes?"

"Yes, Mr. Schmidt."

"What do you know?"

"That you want them."

"Please, Mr. Kelly, do not play games with me. I have offered you a straight proposition."

In the background, behind Mr. Schmidt, apparently not far from the telephone, something screeched. Or squawked. Sam looked quickly over at the bird cage. His own urraca, or rather Anna Jensen's, still crouched or cowered on the bottom of its cage. It had not screeched. The poor bird was terrified speechless. That sound had come over the telephone.

Sam said, "Mr. Schmidt?"

"Yes, Mr. Kelly?"

"I've been reconsidering. Five hundred dollars is not enough retainer for this work that you want me to do for you. We both know that the material you want is police evidence. I don't think I want to involve myself for a paltry five hundred dollars. I would prefer to return your money to you when it arrives tomorrow morning. If you will give me an address . . ."

"Will five thousand suffice as a retainer, sir?"

"Yes."

"You shall have it, another forty-five hundred in the mail. Are you satisfied now, Mr. Kelly?"

"All in cash," Sam said, "used bills, nothing bigger than a twenty."

"I understand."

No, you don't, thought Sam.

# 8

On his way to lunch with Madam Bobbie he stopped by Maria Devincenzi's apartment as he had promised her. There was no answer when he rang the bell, and no answer to his knock, so he went again to the lobby for keys. She had said she was scared. Under his questioning she had said she had no reason to be scared, but she was scared. All right, Sam thought, put it down to feminine nerves. But he had promised to look in on her, and he would do so.

Besides, she had known David Christopher and she had a right to know what had happened to him. She might, in fact, know something about it already, something that would help to find his killer. Maybe she had lied when she said she had no reason to be scared.

There were still a few cops hanging about the lobby, and the usual hotel characters, and apparently word of the second murder had got about, for the Little Old Ladies and Little Old Men had their old gray heads together, gossiping and clucking their righteous indignation.

While he was getting the keys to Devvy's apartment, Sam also picked up the telephone call slips for Anna Jensen's and David Christopher's apartments. He pocketed them, intending to look them over at lunch. And as with the mail for Anna Jensen and David Christopher, he was surprised that Lieutenant Moynihan had not got there first.

Mr. Singh had gone to lunch, and Morris Feigl, the hotel manager, was standing desk duty, so Sam asked him not to mention the call slips to anyone.

"I should tell the cops?" Feigl said. "Cops! They give nothing but trouble! You take what you want, Mr. Kelly. Do your job."

Sam went up to Devvy's apartment again and let himself in. Hers was a studio apartment: bed-sitting room, bathroom, kitchenette, small foyer, and two closets. Sam looked in the bathroom, then the kitchen, finally the closets. No Devvy. He saw the toes of a pair of shoes sticking out from under the bed, and he got down on his hands and knees to have a look. But she was not there either.

Well, Sam thought, maybe she had gone over to Madam Bobbie's place after all, as he had suggested. Or was she on one of the fire-stairs landings with her throat cut?

She had known David Christopher well. But how well? It was he who had brought her to the Hotel Castlereagh in the first place. One night he had wandered down to Chelsea, to a bar called G. J. D'Arcy's. It was a new place, and D'Arcy himself was an old friend. During the evening David spotted this flaming, green-eyed redhead—as he told it later—on a stool at the front end of the bar.

He decided immediately that one way or another he was going to have her. So he asked D'Arcy's permission to speak to her, then took his drink to the front end of the bar and asked her if he might sit by her. She said yes. He asked her if he might buy her a drink. She accepted. Before the drink arrived he asked her if she would come with him to his apartment.

"It's twenty dollars," she said.

"Let's go, then."

"And five more for the taxi to bring me back here," she said.

"Agreed."

They did not wait for their drinks. He left a five on the bar, and they grabbed a cab—a Checker, of course. She didn't go back to G. J. D'Arcy s. Next morning she was still in David Christopher's apartment. By then he had got her life story, and he had offered to introduce her to Madam Bobbie. This got her off the street.

She *had* known David Christopher and known him well. The question now in Sam's mind was *how* she had known him. Had she known what he was into with Anna Jensen? Sam doubted it. For one thing, she hadn't tricked with David lately. He had specialized in streetwalkers, and she was a high-class call girl now. Expensive. If she still stayed at the Hotel Castlereagh it was because Madam Bobbie wanted her nearby, where she could tap her for quickies.

When Sam got back to the lobby he gave Morris Feigl the keys to Devvy's apartment. And on a hunch he asked for the registration record on 14-A, the suite across the hall from his own, where the big brown girl with the magnolia accent lived and where he had smelled marijuana smoke. But just then Mr. Singh came back from his lunch hour, and Feigl turned the problem over to him.

"Who's in Fourteen-A?" Sam asked Mr. Singh.

The Pakistani looked it up in the registration cards.

"Oh, yes," he said, "a young lady, Angela Grandville, from New Orleans. She checked in alone, the third of May, fifty dollars for one week." He grinned at Sam. "Have you seen her, Mr. Kelly? She is the foremost blond woman I have ever seen, sir! Oh, sir, she is truly beyond belief!"

The girl who had opened the door of 14-A when Sam knocked because of marijuana smoke in the hallway was not remotely blond, he was thinking, so he filed that thought away under Future Business and asked for her telephone call slips, or rather for Angela Grandville's. He put them in his pocket with the others.

He left the hotel. The police cordon was still set up. There were also press cars now and a television truck. Reporters and photographers stood around waiting. The camera crew on the traffic island in the middle of Broadway had gone to lunch, leaving two men to guard the equipment and catch any pick-up shots that occurred in the vicinity. An ambulance pulled up in front of the hotel. A black city car stopped alongside it. Dr. James Wu got out and went into the hotel.

Sam stopped on the traffic island and looked around, seeing things from the camera's point of view. He bit down hard on the butt of his cigar, took a box of matches out of his jacket pocket, struck one, and lit the cigar.

"You've been here all morning," he said to the

camera crew. "You must have shot a lot of footage."

One of them looked at him, looked away, and said, "Yeah, pretty good."

"What time did you set up this morning?"

"Early," the man said.

"How early? Do you object to my asking?"

"How early?" the man said. "I don't know. I didn't get here till ten." He turned to his partner. "How early, Fred?"

"Five o'clock," said Fred.

"Thanks," said Sam.

Madam Bobbie was dressed and ready to go when he got to her place. She looked to him as elegant as a Fifth Avenue high-fashion model, with the appreciable difference that they run skinny. She wore a dark blue ankle-length, many-pleated Spanish skirt, scarlet Moroccan leather boots, and a stiffly starched, high-necked white blouse with much lace at the neck. The long blue skirt set off the blue cameo brooch at her throat and the pendant sapphire earrings. Her eyes seemed to glow like sapphires. And with her blond curly hair and peaches-and-cream complexion, Sam thought, she looked good enough to eat. In fact, he proposed something of the sort, but she said she was ravenous for lunch, not having had breakfast.

"How's the weather?"

"Warm," Sam said. "And getting warmer."

"So I'll wear just a stole."

"Just a stole" was a blue fox with pink-dyed mink lining. Now she was all decked out in red, white, and blue. To such a patriotic color combination, Sam thought, one ought to salute or at least stand up and cheer.

While she was getting her stole from the foyer

closet he went to the bedroom and closed and locked the balcony windows. In New York City if you have a balcony or even just a fire escape you also have a standing invitation to cat burglars.

Then he went back into the parlor and spoke to Carlitos. The big bird strutted up and down its perch, cocking a golden eye at him and talking a streak: "Good morning, Sam! Hello, there! What's your name? Pretty bird!" It also spoke some unprintable Spanish.

"Do you want to telephone the hotel before we go?" Madam Bobbie asked.

"I'll call from the restaurant," Sam said.

"So let's go already."

Sam said good-bye to Carlitos.

The big black Mexican magpie screeched.

Taking Madam Bobbie's keys, Sam double-locked, dead-locked, and chain-locked the hall door. Even in the Charmian Towers, with closed-circuit TV surveillance in every hallway, you lock up. After all, who is going to surveille the surveillors? Bobbie had walked on down the hall. She pressed the elevator button.

In the elevator Sam asked her, "How did you happen to get a critter like Carlitos?"

"A client gave him to me. Why?"

"I think I asked you once before, when you first got him," Sam said. "Who did you say gave him to you?"

"Don't be sneaky, Sam."

"Well, who gave him to you?"

"Just a client. You know I don't discuss my clients. Do you talk about yours? I hope not."

"I need to know, Bobbie."

"Why?"

"There's a big black Mexican magpie at the hotel. It belonged to a woman who was murdered there last night."

"So?"

"So how many people in this city have such a bird? Even in Mexico, if people want talking birds they buy parrots or mynahs, not urracas. It's a strange coincidence, which is why I'm asking."

"So it's a coincidence. Who's the dead woman?"

"She's registered as Anna Jensen."

"Never heard of her."

"I didn't think you had, Bobbie. But I think maybe your client has."

"Why? Because of a bird?"

"A very special bird."

They had reached the lobby, and Zebedee Watkins, the giant doorman, was already pushing the button that controlled the street door. He gave Madam Bobbie his widest smile. Sam wondered if Zebedee knew her occupation. Probably. Across the lobby the cold-eyed bell captain and his fishy-eyed bellhops were smirking. Eat your hearts out, Sam was thinking.

"That lousy hotel you live in," Madam Bobbie said when they were on the street. "Full of junkies and God knows what! Some junkie robbed and killed that woman, and you come to me with a lot of bird talk!"

"Agreed," Sam said, "the Hotel Castlereagh is lousy. But it's good enough for you to send your girls there. How come?"

"Because you're there. You know that. I count on you to watch out for them."

She took a pair of black wrap-around sunglasses out of her handbag and put them on. The bag was of scarlet Moroccan leather to match her boots. She looked like a movie queen trying not to be inconspicuous. The camera crew on the traffic island spotted her and swiveled—"panned"—their big machine around to catch her. She did not seem to notice.

"We don't think it was a junkie," Sam said. "Anna Jensen was beaten to death, then her throat was cut. The apartment was tossed, but nothing seems to have been stolen except her keys."

"So what do birds have to do with it?"

"That's what I'd like to find out."

"Sam, the client who gave me that magpie is not the kind of man who beats women to death. He's a gentleman."

"Tell me one thing, Bobbie?"

"Try me."

"Does this gentleman have a magpie himself?"

"I don't know. Why?"

"Can you find out for me?"

"I don't know. I'll have to think about it."

"If he has one, he may be a dangerous man to know, even if he is a gentleman. Think it over."

"Sam, you're trying to pin a murder on someone you don't even know! And I'm not going to help you get my client in trouble! You know, sometimes you act like a cop!"

"Force of habit, honey."

"Well, it's a habit you should break!"

"Can't help it. Right now I'm wondering why this client of yours gave you a Mexican magpie instead of a diamond bracelet."

"Well, I guess it won't do any harm to tell you that much. It was for Valentine's Day."

"A diamond bracelet would seem more appropriate," Sam said.

"He taught the bird a little speech, a valentine, you see, and when the cage was delivered, Carlitos recited the speech. Remember how the Western Union used to have singing telegrams? The delivery boys would stand at your door and sing birthday greetings or whatever? Well, it was like that."

"Everything's up to date in New York City," said Sam.

"Well, that's what happened, Sam."

"Do you think Carlitos could remember the valentine now? It's been three months since you got him—since February."

"He might," Madam Bobbie said. "It was just a simple speech. Let's see, it went something like . . . No, I don't remember. But it was only a few words, a rhyme about *mine* and *valentine*. So try it on him and see what he says."

"I don't think Anna Jensen's urraca sang her a valentine," Sam said.

"Why not?"

"She was a plain jane and a lush. She was also too old for your clients. They only want young women, right?"

"Not all of them. But you're right about Wolfie."

"Wolfie?"

"I shouldn't have said that."

"Tell me about Wolfie."

"Nothing. It's just his nickname."

"Wolfie is short for what?"

"I'm not going to talk about him, Sam!"

"Wolfie! That's cute."

"So glad you like it."

"Now, why would Wolfie give Anna Jensen a Mexican magpie?"

"How do you know he did?"

"I don't, do I? But how many people give these birds as presents? Too much of a coincidence."

"So it's a coincidence. What does that prove?"

"It doesn't prove anything, Bobbie. But it makes me suspicious."

"Once a cop . . . !"

Sam grabbed her arm and swung her around to face him, stopping her there on the street in broad daylight, and kissed her full on the mouth. Out of the corner of his eye he saw that the camera crew had caught it. She struggled a little and hauled off to hit him, but he knew she wouldn't do that.

They had reached the corner of 69th Street and Broadway when the ambulance from in front of the Hotel Castlereagh went howling down Broadway with the Assistant Coroner's black city car behind it.

"David Christopher's in that meat wagon," Sam said.

"What?"

"There were *two* murders, Bobbie."

"Oh, how awful, Sam! Not David!"

"Somebody hung a knife in him."

"Why didn't you tell me?"

"I'm telling you now. Who's Wolfie?"

"Did David have a black magpie too?"

"No. But whoever killed the Jensen woman killed David."

They walked along 69th Street toward the Fleur de Lis, and Madam Bobbie took Sam's arm and hung on tight.

"He was such a nice man," she said. "Why

would anyone . . . ? What was the connection between him and the dead woman, Sam?"

"I don't know yet."

"They must have been into something together, don't you think?"

"You see it right away, honey. Now maybe you'll tell me just a little something about this Wolfie?"

"I don't know what to tell you. I don't know his name. When I met him he said to just call him Wolfie. What he does for a living, I don't know. And I don't know why he sent me that big black bird. But I didn't think about it at the time. At first I took it for a crow, because I know that crows can talk, but when I had a chance to ask Wolfie he said it's called an urraca, related to the magpie."

"Can you get in touch with Wolfie?"

"No, I can't. He calls me when he wants a party. I seldom see him. Usually I send him a girl, or two or three if it's a big party. He always asks for Devvy."

"But at least you've met him. You can describe him."

"Well, he's been to my place a time or two. That's funny, come to think of it—I mean, when he comes around . . ."

"What's funny?"

"Well, he's never been announced from the lobby."

"Maybe he bribes the doorman."

"I don't think so."

Sam said, "The restaurant has its own entrance on the side street, and you can get from the restaurant to the mezzanine lounge and from there to the elevators. Your Wolfie could have come in that way."

"Still, one of the bellmen would have seen him on the television, wouldn't they?"

"Not necessarily. They can't watch all the hallways all the time. And even if they saw him, what would they do? You say he's a gentleman. They wouldn't suspect anything. They'd take him for one of the tenants, right?"

"I guess so. But why would he do that? I mean, why would he come in that way instead of using the lobby?"

"Maybe he doesn't want to be seen in public."

"He must be some kind of big shot."

"I believe he is," Sam said. "But what kind?"

"Now you've got *me* wondering!"

"Good! Keep at it, baby!"

"If I thought Wolfie had anything to do with murder . . . !"

"Tell me, Bobbie. Tell me about Wolfie. Anything you can think of."

"I've told you everything I know. I really don't know anything."

"You said he always asks for Devvy."

"Yes."

"Start there."

"She doesn't talk about her tricks, and I don't ask. Unless there's something wrong. And there was never anything wrong with Wolfie. She would have told me. Ask her yourself. By the way, she quit the life."

"She quit hustling?"

"She took a job in a discothéque just a few days ago. No more dates, she said. But I figure she'll be back."

They had come to the little French restaurant. You have to step down to enter the Fleur de Lis. It occupies the ground floor of an old brownstone. When they came in the maître d'hôtel immediately led them to a table halfway back and against the west wall. He gave them menus and took their order for drinks. Since you never have to reserve a table at the Fleur de Lis the maître d'hôtel seldom knows his customers by name, but if you are a regular he always manages to indicate that he knows you. He knew that Sam and Madam Bobbie always took a table halfway back and against the west wall. Sam didn't have to tell him.

Sam excused himself and went to the telephones. He called the Castlereagh and told Mr. Singh where he would be lunching, then asked for Lieutenant Moynihan. The detective had just returned from his own lunch, and he asked Sam where he was at the moment. Sam told him.

Moynihan said, "I have a few details for you. Do you want it now, or do you want to eat first?"

"Now, Mike."

"Well, the knife in your friend's back has a seven-inch blade, thin, and edged so fine you could shave with it, probably a boning or flensing knife. Wu says he thinks it went straight to the heart and all the way through it. Death would be instantaneous. He was probably asleep when he was hit. Did he ever pass out drunk?"

"Frequently. That's the main reason I was looking in on him, you know—checking him out in the mornings. He drank like there was no tomorrow."

"Well, as you know, there's an empty Jack Daniel's bottle."

"With a lipstick print on one of the drinking glasses," Sam said.

"Maybe one of his girl friends did him in."

"I don't think so. Do you?"

"These girls! They're all renegades!"

"Not all, Mike."

"I have yet to see an honest whore."

"You should get around more. We have some very nice girls in this neighborhood."

"If you say so, Sam, but I'm married, so what do I know? By the way, your friend was killed after the Jensen woman, about two hours later, around six this morning. I thought you'd be interested in that."

"It means the knife that was used to cut Anna Jensen's throat could be the one we found in David's back."

"You make anything of it?"

"I'm not sure. What about the lipstick on the glass?"

"According to Wu, it's probably the Jensen woman's."

"Any fingerprints on the glasses?"

"Not even a smudge."

"Strange."

"What's strange? Whoever made the hit just naturally wiped off any fingerprints. There weren't any on the doorknobs either."

"Mike, if the killer wiped away the fingerprints on the glass he—or she—used . . . It doesn't make sense. Why leave a big, beautiful lipstick print?"

"Yeah," Moynihan said. "Sam, how about I come over to that restaurant and we have a little talk?"

"I'm with a lady. Let's make it Donohue's after five, okay?"

"Make it definite. Five thirty on the dot. See you!"

# LOCATION SHOTS 81

"Maybe you'll have Dr. Wu's report by then?"

"I'll see what I can do."

"Good! And, Mike, ask Dr. Wu about the blood splotches in Anna Jensen's apartment. I'd like to know if all that blood came from her. I have a hunch there may be two blood types. Got it?"

"Got it, Sam. Five thirty at Donohue's."

# 9

Madam Bobbie had taken off her sunglasses and was sipping a vermouth cassis when Sam returned from the telephone. A double Jack Daniel's on the rocks awaited him. He took a good, long pull at it.

"How are things at the hotel?" Bobbie asked.

"Heavy and getting heavier."

Sam took the phone call slips out of his pocket and started riffling through them. Bobbie asked what they were. He told her. She thought about it.

He was only looking for familiar numbers, of course, and not really expecting to find any. He would check out the unfamiliar ones later.

Of the several numbers that David Christopher and Anna Jensen had called yesterday, they had one in common: Trafalgar 3-0244. Sam recognized the Trafalgar number as Kimberly Liquors in the Hotel Ansonia.

Of the several numbers that Angela Grandville had called, Sam had recognized only one—Madam Bobbie's.

"Well," he said, "it's not a total loss." He put the slips away.

"Don't the police want those, Sam?"

"Most likely."

"You could get in trouble that way, couldn't you?"

"I'll try not to."

"Sam, what's wrong?"

"They called me from the hotel last night."

"Oh. I see."

"Why did you switch off your phone, Bobbie?"

"I'm sorry. It's just that I didn't want us to be disturbed. They're always calling you during the night, and all—"

"It's too much for you, baby?"

"I said I'm sorry."

"David wasn't dead when they called me about noise in Anna Jensen's apartment. She was being murdered at that moment, but he wasn't killed until two hours later. If I had got my call, he might still be alive."

"My God, Sam!"

He signaled one of the waitresses and ordered second drinks. They drank in silence for a while. Then the waitress came back for their order. Sole amandine for Bobbie. Filet mignon rare for himself. Chablis for her, burgundy for him. Spinach au gratin. Watercress with oil and vinegar. No dessert, just café filtre and cognac to finish the meal.

The Fleur de Lis is busy on a Friday noon, but it is never crowded at any time. The diners are mostly West Siders—professionals of various kinds, writers and editors, actors and actresses, merchants—people who will pay seven or ten dollars for lunch but not twenty. Madison Avenue and the garment center do not bring their credit cards this far uptown, though the Fleur de Lis is an old restaurant, authentically French and well established by time. It is frequented by the French themselves. The kitchen crew and the waitresses are all French. It is not an elegant restaurant. If you want elegance for lunch, you go midtown to the "Frog Pond," as the credit-card set affectionately call La Grenouille, or to Orsini's—where the waiters act as if you were visiting aristocracy—the prices are much higher, and the food is no better than you get at the Fleur de Lis.

"You've never switched off your telephone before," Sam said. "I mean, when I've stayed overnight."

"Yes, I have," said Bobbie. "This is just the first time I've been caught at it."

"But you don't do it every time."

"I wish I hadn't done it this time, Sam. Believe me, I feel awful about it! I liked your friend David, and I'd do anything in the world—"

"Let's not talk about it, Bobbie."

"Of course," she said. Then, "Did you know he sent me a few girls? He said he wanted to see them get off the street."

"I knew about Devvy," said Sam. "I didn't know he'd sent you others."

"Several—Freddie, Gwen, Judy . . ."

"Greater love hath no man," Sam said. "He priced them right out of his bracket, didn't he?"

"Not exactly," Bobbie said. "They kept in touch with him. They made sure he got what he wanted. I've heard more than one of them say she loved him. He was a nice man."

"I know," Sam said. "But I guess I didn't know

him as well as I thought I did."

"By the way," Bobbie said, "Devvy quit the life."

"So you said. And she took a job in a discothéque."

"Now that she isn't hustling, I suppose you'll be after her," Bobbie said.

"She's a very beautiful girl," Sam said.

"Men!"

"Which disco? Did she say?"

"It's called Raven."

"Interesting."

"Like I thought, you do have eyes for that wop!"

"Bobbie," said Sam, "tell me about Angela Grandville."

"How do you know about *her?*"

"It's my business to know. I'm the hotel dick at the Castlereagh, remember?"

"She came up from New Orleans. What do you want to know?"

"And her girl friend?"

"They call her Big Babe," said Bobbie. "Also from New Orleans. Why do you ask?"

"Just curious, honey. I'm wondering why you didn't tell me you had a couple of new girls at the hotel."

"No reason. Does it matter?"

"I don't know. I hope not."

"Sam, you're getting paranoid."

"Paranoid, is it? A double killing at the hotel, my best friend murdered, and I'm getting paranoid."

# 10

It was nearly two o'clock when they finished lunch, which they managed to do without further reference to the night's events at the Hotel Castlereagh. After cognac and café filtre Madam Bobbie wanted Sam to come back up to her apartment for a matinee, but he insisted on taking her straight to the Chase Manhattan Bank as usual. One of his chores as a private detective was to escort certain persons to the bank, or sometimes to make the run by himself. Madam Bobbie banked on Fridays and Mondays regularly. Luncheon was customary on these days, usually at the Fleur de Lis but occasionally at the Casa Delmonte on 72nd Street or at Victor's on Columbus Avenue.

Their nights together were less regular and depended on who called whom. Sam did not know and did not want to know when she had other arrangements. She said she did not turn tricks herself, and he accepted that. However, of late he had been rather disturbed to notice that she was beginning to question the time he spent apart from her. Callhouse madam though she was, the nesting instinct ran true to form in her, he thought, alarmingly true to form, and it was a development he did not welcome.

"I've got business to take care of this afternoon," he told her. "Maybe I'll call you tonight."

"Maybe I'll be home," she said.

It was only a short walk to the Chase Manhattan on Amsterdam, next to the new synagogue. She made her deposit and paid him his fifty-dollar fee. Then he took her back to the Charmian Towers, kissed her at the street door, and thanked her for lunch, which she had, of course, charged to her American Express account. From each according to his ability, he thought, to each according to his need.

That bank deposit, he had observed, came to fourteen hundred dollars, and it represented somewhat less than the total sum of monies earned for her since Monday by her stable of girls. She would likely do as well over the weekend. She did not get to keep all the loot, of course, for out of these sums she paid a high rent (twenty-five hundred a month), a lawyer's retainer, and a certain politician's graft. Still, Madam Bobbie could afford lunch at the Fleur de Lis.

She was not Sam's only client. There was a gentleman who lived in the old Majestic Apartments at Central Park West and 72nd Street, where Costello had been shot, and from time to time Sam picked up an extra hundred by escorting this gentleman to or from a small airport in New Jersey. He didn't know the details—it was enough that the gent needed a man with a gun and the license to carry it and that he paid well for a couple of hours' work. One hundred dollars a run was good pay, according to Sam, though he sometimes wondered whether his client would agree to raise the rate if a shooting war broke out.

And there was a fat shark who operated out of a low-life saloon over on Columbus Avenue but lived in a high-life apartment house on 72nd Street and sometimes required an escort, especially on Friday evenings when he had made good collections. He paid fifty dollars a run, and Sam took the fifty with the feeling that he was being overpaid. The man's life was not, he felt, worth that much. In fact, the neighborhood had any number of people who would smile the night some television newscaster announced the timely demise of one Max Shapiro. The right man could do the community a public service. Irony, irony, Sam often said to himself, all is irony and chasing after the buck.

The manager of a card room on 79th Street called him too from time to time, whenever too much money got in the game, and this was another fifty-dollar fee that could be counted on about once a week. The money might not be strictly legal, but at least it was clean.

And Sam did a small business with legitimate merchants, though it was irregular, as when one of them would require the services of an armed man to protect the extra-large sums brought in by a fire sale.

Sam was also on call for rougher kinds of private police work, should trouble develop in any of the bordellos, card rooms, crap games, or other such entertainments in the neighborhood. Sam could do for these enterprises what a regular cop could not. Or would not. Or might not. With Sam you were safe: he would quell the trouble, take his fee, and nothing more.

But you had better be right if you called him. Everybody who was anybody in the high life on the West Side remembered the time a big whoremaster on Riverside Drive had had some trouble in his bordello and called Sam Kelly. Sam came running, thinking he was needed to protect the girls from a dumper or some other freak. What he found was that the girls needed to be protected from their own whoremaster. This creep and some of his buddies had been robbing the girls, taking all the money they earned and actually holding them prisoner in the house, a case of real white slavery. So the girls were staging a riot. They had barricaded themselves in one of the rooms and were doing their best to wreck the place, smashing windows and generally raising enough of a ruckus to attract official police attention if they were not stopped.

This whoremaster must have been pure crazy to think that Sam would help him in a thing like this. But he did have enough sense to realize that the girls would listen to Sam, for Sam Kelly's reputation among the neighborhood frails was like that. They liked him, respected him, and would do what he asked. They knew they could count on him when they needed help.

When he saw what was happening, he put the whoremaster and his buddies under the gun and turned the girls loose on them. Afterward the girls packed up and got out. He sent a couple of the lookers to Madam Bobbie and the others down to the Hotel Castlereagh.

But that was not all. Leaving the whoremaster's

buddies where they lay, he took the creep himself outside at gunpoint, put him in a gypsy cab, got in with him, and rode him down to Roosevelt Hospital. By the time they got to the hospital this creep was ready for the doctors. He had a broken jaw, a gouged eye, a cracked spine, and various internal injuries. How much of this was Sam's work and how much the girls' is a moot point.

Sam gave the creep's wallet to the gypsy cab driver and sent him on his way happy. None of it got into the newspapers, but word spread around the neighborhood because the girls were grateful and said so.

The creep's buddies were found later and buried. There was a brief police investigation, but nothing came of it. What happened was generally known at the precinct, of course, but no one was willing to stand up as a witness. Certainly not the girls themselves. As for the big-shot creep, when he limped out of the hospital several weeks later, he limped right on out of town.

Then there was the time they found a body on the roof of a six-floor brownstone next to the Hotel Castlereagh. It was identified by police as a much-arrested rape suspect. The cops had long been convinced of this degenerate's guilt, and numbers of young women had made complaints against him, but the law requires witnesses. The rapist had therefore been getting away with it until one night he apparently tried it in the Castlereagh. It was said around the West Side that Sam Kelly had caught this freak, walked him to the top of the hotel at gunpoint, and backed him off the roof, which is seventeen floors up. The freak landed on top of the brownstone next door, an eleven-story fall. Maybe

Sam had done it, maybe not. But he got credit for it.

And so he was well known around the West Side. And well liked except by pimps, junkies, muggers, and sundry trash of that sort. His stocky figure, always dressed to the nines, topped by that yellow straw boater in spring, summer, and fall, and by a fine black Italian fedora in winter, was a welcome sight to those who had no reason to fear him. And those who had reason learned to stay out of his way. From time to time newcomers to the neighborhood would try him—hoodlums and hooligans from outside, from the Bronx, or Brooklyn, the Lower East Side or Harlem—but they never tried twice. He carried his Astra .25 "Cub" automatic rather than a heavier weapon like the Colt .45 or an S & W .38 because he was not likely to kill with it unless he chose to. He could place one of those little .25 copper-jacketed bullets wherever he wanted it without fear of tearing too big a hole. He could put it in a man's kneecap and cripple him, or in his shoulder, without utterly destroying the man. Of course, he could also place the shot in the man's head if he chose.

He felt good after lunch with Madam Bobbie, but just a little over-full, so he went for a leisurely stroll, stopping at the Off-Track Betting office on 72nd Street to lay a sawbuck on the nose of Sweetie Pie at 20–1 in the seventh at Belmont. While he was in the O.T.B. office he spotted a numbers man who lived in the Castlereagh and put five on the day's digits. Then he walked east on 72nd Street and into Central Park. All the women and dogs and old men were out sunning themselves. And apparently school was out or the entire student population of New York City was playing hookey, for there were hundreds, maybe thousands of Puerto Rican and black kids around the big fountain at the lower end of the lake. Many were out in rowboats. Some were clustered in groups with bongos, congas, and even a few horns. The noise was deafening. The fragrance of marijuana smoke was everywhere. There were a few narcotics cops from the 20th Precinct, trying to look like hippies, but Sam knew they would not dare try an arrest. They would be mobbed, beaten, maybe killed. As it was, he saw no violence, only a little rowdiness, boys pushing each other into the lake, no harm done. He walked down by the Sheep Meadow and watched the kite fliers for a while. There was just enough movement in the air, not a wind, not a breeze, more like a zephyr, so that you had to be really good to get a kite up. A couple of soccer teams were kicking a ball around. A softball game was going. Young lovers were lying about, some with guitars. And all kinds of dogs were frolicking with great gusto, Danes and dachshunds, shepherds and schnauzers, and just plain mutts.

In a way, Sam wished he had gone with Madam Bobbie to her apartment for a matinee. But this thing about her telephone put him off. And not just the telephone.

There was also that big black Mexican magpie. Was it mere coincidence that she and Anna Jensen both had one? Parrots, yes, or mynahs, cockatoos, budgies—but urracas?

Moreover, it would seem that one Richard Schmidt also had such a bird, for it had undoubtedly been an urraca that had screeched over the phone when Sam and Schmidt had been discussing their deal.

There was more than coincidence in these birds,

Sam felt sure. There was a pattern if he could only read it, like the unifying motif in the design of an Oriental carpet.

If birds could only talk!

But mimicry is not speech.

# 11

Returning to the Castlereagh, he found that the squad cars and the police cordon were gone from in front of the hotel and the lobby was normal again. Or as normal as the Castlereagh lobby ever was. At least there were no cops.

He went up to his own apartment, put the tea kettle on, and got ready to steam open David Christopher's and Anna Jensen's letters. He put his boater on the hat rack, hung his jacket in the foyer closet, and unbuttoned his vest. He felt like having a shot, so he poured a good one and took a sip, straight, then another. He got a fresh cigar out of the box, bit off the tip, and lit up. The tea kettle started whistling. He removed the whistle from the spout.

Baudelaire came out from under the bed then, and Sam picked him up and cradled him in his arms and spoke soft nonsense to him. Then he put him down on the floor and checked his food and water. There was plenty of both.

He took a look at the big black Mexican magpie. It seemed to have recovered. It was perched on a crossbar of its cage, looking about the room with a golden stare. Its food and water containers were full.

None of the plants needed watering.

Steaming open David Christopher's and Anna Jensen's letters was the work of a mere minute. When he had them open he sat by the windows and examined the contents.

David had only one letter. It was from a Madison Avenue lawyer who specialized in literary and other entertainment law, writing contracts for authors, composers, television executives, performers, and the like. This letter concerned several bits of outstanding business—a lawsuit against a hardcover publisher who had apparently been falsifying royalty reports, an investigation into a paperback publisher's deal with the same hardcover publisher, and negotiations for a television deal concerning dramatic rights on David's early Western stories, written before he had turned to science books for children. Sam could see nothing in all this that might tie in with his friend's murder.

But there was a postscript. It read as follows:

> You must not show the manuscript about the mutual-fund swindle to editors until I have checked it. As for this swindler's Nazi past, how much can you trust his wife's testimony? I ought to audition those tapes, don't you think?

Anna Jensen had only one letter. It was from the Chase Manhattan Bank informing her that the remaining securities she had left with them had been sold and the money credited to her account. The sum was thirty thousand dollars, less commission, giving a new balance of eighty thousand three hundred seventy-nine dollars and forty cents. The branch manager added the information that if Miss Jensen had other securities she would like him to handle he was at her service. Furthermore, if she would care to discuss ways of investing her money he was always available for consultation.

The envelope was addressed to Miss Anna Jensen, which seemed strange to Sam, for he thought he remembered her wearing a plain gold band on her third finger, left hand. But he was not certain.

According to the letterhead, the telephone for the Chase Manhattan branch was 552-1185. He got out the telephone call slips for David and Miss Jensen. Both had called that number yesterday. So they both had business at the same bank branch. Was it the same business? Not securities, certainly, for David was not into that kind of money. He'd been having trouble collecting his rightful royalties. Still, he and the Jensen woman could have something else together at the bank. Well, he would think about that later.

He got a small bottle of mucilage out of his desk and resealed the letters, then took another sip from his glass of whiskey. He had all the facts he needed, he was sure of it, but they were like a jigsaw puzzle: the assembled picture would show Mexican magpies, keys, stock securities, a manuscript, some tape recordings—and what else? No, it did not matter what else. With all this, he had enough. The only question was how to assemble the pieces of the puzzle.

He went to the bird cage. The big black urraca

looked at him, did a quick shuffle on the crossbar, and muttered deep in its throat.

He tried several words on it: *Wolfie, Anna, David, Bobbie, murder, help*. None of these made it respond. He tried a few common expressions in Spanish: *Viva México! Y los hijos de la chingada! Salud! Pesetas! Amor! Y tiempo para gastarlas!*

Suddenly the big black bird said, "Jay!" It squawked and again said, "Jay!" Then it said, "*Hilf mir!* Jay! *Hilf mir!*" Once it got going it spoke very clearly, including the German words, for, after all, the magpie speaks no language. It mimics.

And then it screamed. Not a squawk this time, not a screech like the cry made by Madam Bobbie's urraca. It was more like the kind of scream that a woman would make.

## 12

The Central Savings Bank time-and-temperature sign over Verdi Square said 5:30 and 70 degrees when Sam went down to the lobby. At the desk Mr. Singh told him that Lieutenant Moynihan had asked for Anna Jensen's and David Christopher's mail and for their telephone call slips.

"I told him no letters and no call slips for yesterday," Mr. Singh said. "I hope I did right, Mr. Kelly. I didn't want to get you in trouble."

"You did fine, Terry," said Sam. "Has Mr. Saul Braun come home yet?"

"I am Saul Braun," said a voice behind him.

Turning, he saw one of the Little Old Men and recognized him. Saul Braun was one of the very few who still went to the office. A cutter in the garment center since he first came to this country, he could have retired long ago to Florida or to Israel, but he was the type that thrives on work and perishes without it. He was a smiling little yidl with bright blue eyes, fair skin, and a nose like a fish hawk's.

"Mr. Braun," said Sam, "I'm the house detective."

"I know who you are, Mr. Kelly," said Mr. Braun. "So you want to ask me about last night, or this morning? It was four o'clock already."

"Yes. Well, what exactly did you hear, Mr. Braun?"

"Yelling and screaming is what I heard."

"A woman and a man?"

"That's right."

"Do you remember what they said?"

"Will I ever forget? Oy, gewalt!"

"Anything in particular?"

"Like what, Mr. Kelly?"

"Maybe you didn't know, Mr. Braun. The woman across the hall from you was murdered around the time you called the desk to complain about noise coming from her apartment."

"They told me at work today," Mr. Braun said. "Somebody came to me this morning. It was that upstairs Levy from the showroom. He said, 'Saul, they killed a woman at your hotel last night.' So I said to myself, 'Saul, you were listening to a murder and you didn't know it!' Such a hotel! Yech!"

"Mr. Braun," said Sam, "please try to remember what the man said, or what the woman said. Anything at all."

"The woman said, 'I'll kill you! I'll kill you! You lousy, rotten so-and-so!'"

"So-and-so?"

"Well, she said something stronger." Mr. Braun looked around the lobby, cupped a hand to his mouth, and spoke softly, almost whispering. "She said son of a bitch and some other things worse."

"You said *she* was threatening to kill *him?*"

"That's right."

"Did she at any time call him by name?"

"You mean like Heinrich or Karl, maybe?"

"Yes."

"No. But he called her Anna."

"Did you hear either of them say anything that might indicate what they were quarreling about?"

"Yes. She had something he wanted. He kept asking her for it. I can't remember . . . Yes, now I remember. Some kind of records, I think, and some papers—securities, stocks or bonds or something like that. He was saying, 'I want those securities.' And she was saying, 'You owe me more than that, you lousy so-and-so!' He said she stole them from him, and she said he stole them from somebody else. She laughed at him and she said, 'How can a woman steal from her own husband?'"

"Thank you, Mr. Braun," said Sam. "Now tell me, was there anything distinctive about the man's voice or speech? Did he have a Swedish accent?"

"Swedish?"

"Jensen is a Swedish name."

"No, Mr. Kelly. He was German. They were both Germans. Not only Germans, they were Prussians! Believe me, I should know!"

"You're from Germany yourself, Mr. Braun?"

The little man pulled up the sleeve of his jacket just enough to show some small blue numbers tattooed on the wrist. In Germany he had been 746006.

"I was a cutter in Berlin before the war," he said. "My wife and all my family were killed in Belsen. The Nazis did not kill me because I was useful. I cut uniforms for the Prussian officers."

"Thank you, Mr. Braun," said Sam. "You've been very helpful."

"Don't thank me, Mr. Kelly. Just get that lousy Prussian!"

"You may count on it."

"Come to my factory, Mr. Kelly. I'll cut you such a suit! I'll cut you suits for life! Only get that lousy Prussian!"

# 13

When Sam got to Donohue's it was close to six o'clock. Lieutenant Moynihan was not there.

Dennis, the afternoon man, said, "How are you, Mr. Kelly?" as he reached for the bottle of Jack Daniel's.

He poured a double on the rocks. You do not have to *order* a double at Donohue's when Dennis is on duty. In fact, when this fine Irish lad is behind the bar you cannot afford to drink at home.

Sam asked him if there had been any phone calls, and Dennis said, "I was about to tell you, Mr. Kelly. A man named Mike called about twenty minutes ago. He said to tell you Mike called and he would call back later."

Sam thanked him and took a long pull at his drink.

"I guess you've heard about David," he said.

"It was on the radio. A terrible thing! He was a nice man. The drinks are on me, Mr. Kelly."

Sam thanked him again and finished the whiskey

with one more long pull. Dennis replenished the glass, to the brim, and indicated it was on the house again.

"Your health," Sam said and took a smaller pull this time.

"I remember how your friend would sing the 'Cruiskeen Lan'," said Dennis. "But he wasn't Irish, was he?"

"No," Sam said. "Greek."

"Greek?"

"Born in Piraeus."

"Funny, he didn't look Greek."

"You should have heard him sing Greek songs. He and I would get into a bottle and sing all night."

"Well, it's a shame a nice man like that should get murdered. Do you know how it happened, Mr. Kelly? The news reports don't give the details, and the boys who dropped in this afternoon didn't know much about it. Some of them figured it was one of those junkie killings."

"It was not a junkie murder," Sam said. "We're sure of that much."

The bar phone rang and Dennis went to answer it. A couple of vice-squad detectives came in and sat by the front end of the bar. They nodded to Sam. He ignored them. The six-o'clock radio newscast came on then, and the first item was the double murder at the Castlereagh. According to the newscaster, a junkie named Rodney Harrison had been arrested. Sam recognized the name. Rodney was the young junkie punk who had elbowed the Little Old Lady aside when she was about to enter the elevator on the ninth floor. Sam, on his way to check his friend David, had told the punk to get his ass out of the hotel. So Detective Commander

Fuseli had arrested Rodney the punk for the murders of Anna Jensen and David Christopher. And it was Commander Fuseli who had said he did not believe the junkie theory. What then? Had he picked up this punk in order to throw a smoke screen over the case? If so, perhaps he was on the same trail Sam was following. Sam did not like that thought. The D.C. could easily louse up the case. In fact, he was sure to louse it up.

Dennis came back then and said Mike was on the phone. Sam went and took the call.

"I'm at Mrs. J's Sacred Cow," said Moynihan. "We can talk better here."

"Right," Sam said. "I'll head over there. See you in a few minutes."

He went back to his drink, tossed off the rest of it, and thanked the barman again. On his way out the two vice-squad cops spoke to him.

"Sorry to hear about your friend Christopher," one of them said.

And the other said, "He was playing around with prosses, wasn't he?"

"This wasn't a pross killing," Sam said.

"He played around with hookers, though," the first vice cop said.

"I wouldn't put anything past those broads," the second cop said. "They'd knife their own mothers."

"Haven't you heard?" Sam said. "Detective Commander Fuseli picked up a junkie."

"Fuseli!" said the first cop. "Don't make me laugh!"

"You boys have a nice night," Sam said, and he went on out.

From the public phone on the street outside Donohue's he called the Castlereagh and told the switchboard operator he would be at Mrs. J's Sacred Cow for the next hour or so.

As he walked along 72nd Street toward the Sacred Cow the sunset over the Jersey palisades was a blaze of crimson and gold and the sky overhead was deep blue. The hook-and-ladder from the firehouse down Amsterdam Avenue was clanging and shrieking hell-bent uptown for the West Side's slum areas of the Eighties.

When he reached the Sacred Cow he found the cocktail-hour crowd in full cry. They stood three deep at the bar. Cathleen was behind the stick, and a prettier colleen you would go far to find, or a nicer one. Like Dennis at Donohue's when Cathleen is working the bar you can't afford to drink at home. Sam greeted her and she smiled her Irish smile, both hands busily mixing four different cocktails at one time.

Sam saw Mike in a booth at the back and went to join him. One reason for going to Mrs. J's Sacred Cow is the amiable fact that the barmaid and the waitresses work in leotards and sheer black panty hose, and they are all very pretty women and well stacked. Talented too. Some are actresses filling in between engagements, some are singers, one is a school-teacher moonlighting. About half are career waitresses. The food is good too, but Sam did not often go there to eat. He frequented the place because he liked the way Cathleen poured and he liked to watch her while he drank.

Of course, Lieutenant Moynihan chose it as a meeting place for another reason, with which Sam had to agree. Had he considered the problem himself, he would have made his appointment with Moynihan at the Sacred Cow instead of Donohue's.

If you must have a conference with a cop, you are best off at the Cow, for the clients are so square, so straight, neither crooks nor cops, that they will never give you a second look. At Donohue's, however, among a lot of "off-duty" cops, you had to be careful. The fact is that cops are never off duty. They will spy on their brother officers and they will eavesdrop. More, if you are drinking in a fuzz joint, you shouldn't even use the phone, or if you do, you should say nothing.

"I've ordered you a double Jack Daniel's on the rocks," Lieutenant Moynihan said as Sam sat down.

"You're new in the neighborhood," Sam told him, "so let me pull your coat. If the barmaid knows you, you don't have to *ask* for doubles. Her name is Cathleen. Next time you come in she'll remember seeing you with me. You're a member of the club now."

"She's a beauty," Moynihan said. "Irish too, isn't she?"

"That she is, Mike."

"Bedad, they're *all* beauties in this place! It's better than a Playboy Club."

"Absolutely no comparison. Cigar?"

Moynihan accepted a panatela. "Hundred dollars a box, eh?" he said.

"Right."

"That's what *you* pay?"

"Yes."

"You wouldn't need an assistant in your work, Sam? I'm not fussy."

"You wouldn't leave the force now," Sam said. "You're too close to retirement."

"Don't be too sure," Moynihan said. "You're talking to a very discontented cop.

"What's your beef?"

"Detective Commander Gerard Fuseli."

"Understood," Sam said. "Would you feel better if *you* got promoted to detective commander?"

"I should live so long. But enough about me. Let's talk about *you*. I've been making a few discreet inquiries. You've got one hell of a reputation in the Twentieth Precinct. They tell me that whenever they have to go to the Hotel Castlereagh the first person they want to question is you. Either you did it, whatever it is, or you know who did it. That about right, Sam?"

"Well, I'm the hotel dick there. I ought to know what's going on, right?"

"Right. And that's why the D.C. wonders about you. He thinks you know something about this case and you're not telling him."

"What does he care? I hear on the radio that he arrested a junkie punk named Rodney."

"That's just in case we don't get whoever really did it," Moynihan said.

"Then he's not throwing up a smoke screen?"

"What do you mean?"

"He's not on the track of the killer?"

"Fuseli? That's funny! He couldn't catch a kid stealing apples. He couldn't even catch a cold. And you know it."

"Well," Sam said, "maybe *you* can solve the case. I've got something for you." He took Anna Jensen's and David Christopher's letters and their telephone call slips out of his jacket pocket and gave them to Moynihan. "The desk clerk didn't know about these, Mike."

"Didn't, eh?" Moynihan said as he took them. "All right, if you say so, he didn't know. Maybe I should have asked *you* for them in the first place. Anything else, Holmes?"

"Well," Sam said, "I have a theory about the missing keys."

"Shoot."

"Anna Jensen's and David Christopher's apartments were both thoroughly searched. In both cases their keys are missing. Now, let's suppose, for the sake of my theory, that David and the Jensen woman were into something together, something that involved the missing keys. Whoever took one set of keys wouldn't need the other set, right?"

"Right."

"Maybe, Mike. And maybe not. There's a type of safe-deposit box that requires *two* keys to open it."

"I think you might have something there," Moynihan said. He had been casually examining the letters that Sam had given him. He tapped the one from Chase Manhattan with his forefinger. "I'll start with that Chase branch by the Hotel Castlereagh. Thanks for the tip."

"I hope you don't have to give it to the D.C.," said Sam. "He could easily louse it up for you."

"I'll have to give it to him, but not right away," Moynihan said. "Now let me ask you a question. Did your friend David Christopher use his tape recorder for playing music, or was it for dictation?"

"So you noticed the tapes were missing," Sam said.

"Why didn't *you* mention it, Sam?"

"Good question."

"I'd like an answer."

"I'll try to think of one, Mike."

"You're out to solve this case yourself, is that it?"

Sam had left his hat on, as he often did in bars

when he was wearing the boater. Now he took it off, hung it on the hat rack, plucked an Irish linen kerchief out of his left hip pocket, unfolded it, and wiped the sweat off his bald pate.

"I want the man who killed my friend," he said.

Moynihan said, "I'd feel the same way, Sam. Now tell me about the tape recorder."

"You guessed it," Sam said. "David used the machine for dictation. So you might find the missing tapes in that safe-deposit box unless whoever got the two sets of keys has already been to the bank."

"Any idea what's on the tapes?"

"I assume they have something to do with murder. But no, I have no idea what's on them. Have you questioned Saul Braun?"

"That's the man who made the noise complaint last night," Moynihan said. "No, I haven't. Have you?"

"Yes. He heard quite a lot, it seems. Anna Jensen and some man were quarreling. Something about stolen securities. Braun says he heard her yell curses at the man. She claimed a wife could not steal from her husband."

Moynihan had finished looking through the letter from the Chase Manhattan Bank to Anna Jensen.

"Looks like we've got something here," he said.

"There's more," Sam said. "You handle this right, Mike, and you'll retire as detective commander. Now hear this. Saul Braun remembers something else about that quarrel between Anna Jensen and whoever the man was. He thinks they were Germans—in fact, Prussians. Now, Braun is a German Jew. He was 746006 in a concentration camp, and he says he knows the Prussian accent.

Well, Jensen isn't a very German name. It's more Swedish. She could have changed her name, of course, but she couldn't change her accent. I didn't know her well, but I do recall noticing that her accent didn't fit her name. I thought nothing of it—she could have married a Swede, right?"

"I can check that out," Moynihan said. "Her fingerprints would be on file with the Bureau of Immigration and Naturalization. I think we're going to wrap this one up, Sam."

"I know we are."

"I owe you."

"Then let me know what you find out about the fingerprints, will you?"

"Well, I don't know if I can do that, Sam. It's police business."

"Mike!"

"All right! All right! But keep it under your hat. The D.C. would just love to get something on me. He knows I hate his guts."

"Welcome to the club. I've hated the son of a bitch for years. I'd like to put him out of business."

"That bad, eh?"

"I'll tell you about it if you like. It's a rotten story to tell over dinner, though. Did you plan to eat here?"

"No. The wife's expecting me," Moynihan said. "I'll be a little late getting up to the Bronx, but I'd like to hear about you and the D.C."

Sam hailed a waitress and ordered another round. His cigar had gone out. He lit it again and puffed meditatively for a moment.

"Mike," he said, "I don't know why you joined the department, but I'd guess it was for the usual reasons: back from a war, no jobs available, no skills even if the jobs were there, nothing to offer an employer but military training, discipline, and some knowledge of gunnery. So you join the force. Right?"

"That was just about it," Moynihan said. "Mine was the Second World War. Yours must have been Korea."

"I was lucky," Sam said. "I did occupation duty in Germany. But it was the same old story anyway. There was nothing for me when I got back from Europe, and I had a wife to support, so I took the only thing I could get. At first I liked being a police officer. Well, I was twenty years younger then, and wearing the uniform made me feel bigger than a man. Besides, being a cop then was different from what it means now. Patrolmen really patrolled. Now they're headhunters looking for an excuse to make a bust so they can get that extra pay for appearing in court. I was a good cop. No graft, no grift, not even a free cup of coffee at the corner luncheonette. I kept a clean beat. Then one night I got lucky. I just happened to see a heroin deal going down, right on the street, and I made the bust singlehanded. Two big dealers and their gunsels. So they made a detective out of me and put me on the narcotics detail. That's how I first met Detective Commander Gerard Fuseli. He was Lieutenant Fuseli then. I worked under him."

"That explains it," Moynihan said. "You had to work under him. No wonder you hate him."

"No," Sam said. "That wasn't the problem. I'm getting to it. I'd been working with Fuseli a couple of years when one morning he calls the squad into his office and informs us that he has set up a big cocaine deal. This he has managed to do without our knowing about it. Now he needs us to help him make the bust. There were these two Cuban exiles, big coke dealers from before the Cuban revolution, and somehow Fuseli had got to them. If I had known then what I know now, Mike, I would have copped out somehow. I would have seen trouble coming. There was no way Fuseli could have conned a couple of big coke dealers. They would have seen through him right away. Know what I mean?"

"Sure," Moynihan said. "He might get the prices right, but how could he do the tasting himself? They'd spot him for a phony as soon as he took his first snort. He wouldn't understand that. So what happened? I think I can guess."

"The deal went down like this," Sam said. "There would be two adjoining hotel suites. The two Cubans would be in one with the cocaine. Fuseli and one man would be in the other with the money. Now, hear this: one hundred twenty thousand dollars for twenty pounds of pure coke! Dig it?"

Moynihan said, "Who would ever have thought our own Gerry Fuseli knew such big shots?"

"You see the point," Sam said. "That much weight just isn't handled that way. As I say, if I had known then what I know now . . . Anyhow, I went along like a lamb to the slaughter."

"I think I remember the case," Moynihan said. "It was about ten years ago."

"That's right. It was the summer of 'sixty-two."

"A cop was killed?"

"You've got it. Well, Fuseli was really running the game even though he didn't know the name of the game. You know, and I know now, the name of the game was Rip-Off. Of course, those two bastard Cubans never had a chance of getting out of that hotel with the money. Likewise, Fuseli wasn't about to get his hands on twenty pounds of cocaine, either. All right, Fuseli and a young cop named Coogan checked into the hotel with a suitcase full of flash money. I was stationed in a nearby suite with several other men. The two Cubans checked into their suite, next to Fuseli's. The door between was opened. Fuseli flashed the money. And at this point the Cubans explained that the cocaine was downstairs in a car in the hotel garage. One of them would stay upstairs with Fuseli's man and the money while the other would go with Fuseli down to the garage. At this point Fuseli should have put guns on those two characters. He should have known something was going wrong with the deal. But not Gerry Fuseli. He was a mastermind. Well, as soon as he and this Cuban left the suite to go down to the garage and get the coke, the shooting started. Young Coogan got a forty-five slug in the head, blowing his brains all over the room. The rest of us came out of hiding then, and we liquidated both Cubans, but not before two of us caught bullets. I got mine in the left foot. Another cop got his in the chest. It went through a lung and lodged next to his spine, paralyzing him from the arms down and for life. Fuseli didn't get a scratch. He didn't get the cocaine either. There wasn't any. Never had been. It was a rip-off all the way. And here's the pay-off: even though the whole deal went sour and cost the life of a good man and permanently crippled another, Lieutenant Fuseli got promoted to detective commander. And that, Mike, is why I quit the force. It is also why I would like to put Fuseli out of business. I'm sure young Coogan would agree, and so would the cop who was paralyzed."

"I can see how you feel," Moynihan said. "Did you get a pension for the foot wound?"

"No. It wasn't bad enough for that. I could have stayed on the force."

"Well, Fuseli hasn't changed, Sam. He's still a mastermind."

"I can see that. Tell me, do you have to give everything to him? I mean, can you hold out on him, maybe solve this case yourself, score off him? I'd like to help you do that. Maybe I can. Care to try?"

"No dice," Moynihan said. "I go by the book. But thanks anyway. I appreciate the gesture."

"Nevertheless," Sam told him, "if I get anything else, I'll pass it on to you, not to the D.C."

"And I'll be thanking you, Sam. And I'll hate it just as much as you, seeing Fuseli take the credit."

"Well, it's just possible he won't get the credit this time."

"Are you trying to tell me something?"

Running his hand over his bald head, Sam looked as if he was about to tell the man something, but then he shrugged, smiled a small smile, and said, "Maybe it's a little too soon. What about the lipstick on the drinking glass in David's apartment?"

Moynihan said, "Like I told you on the phone, Wu says it's the same brand and color as the Jensen woman's. That doesn't mean much. Lots of broads use the same brand."

"True, Mike, but it fits. I'm sure you found her fingerprints in David's apartment and his in hers. Five will get you ten it's her lip print on the glass."

"So she was drinking with him last night. Where does that get us?"

"First the facts, Mike, then the theory. Right?"

"Right. Here's another fact for you. There were *two* blood types in the Jensen woman's apartment. Most of the blood was hers, of course, but there were a few drops of another blood type."

"Probably the killer's," Sam said. "Have you questioned Jay Murphy, the night clerk?"

"Not yet. Have *you?*"

"No."

"Well, unless you have something else for me, it's time I got started for the Bronx."

Sam introduced Moynihan to Cathleen, the barmaid, on their way out. She said she had heard about David Christopher's death and felt very sad about it. "He was such a nice man!" She asked for details, but Sam said he did not know what the police were doing about it except that a junkie had been arrested.

He left Moynihan in front of the Sacred Cow, promising to get in touch tomorrow, and watched the big mick walk east toward Broadway and the IRT subway's 72nd Street express stop, where he would board a train for the Bronx, his wife, dinner, and an evening of television. Sam envied him, remembering how it had been before his wife died. And for a moment loneliness gripped him. Well, he would stop in at W. M. Tweed's for a quick one, a pain killer. Solomon said money answereth all things, but he was wrong: bourbon answereth all things.

Sam headed west from Mrs. J's Sacred Cow, stopping in at the stationer's for the *Post* and the *News*.

At Tweed's he found Frankie behind the bar. She was a very lovely Cuban of Spanish blood and not mestiza, and when she was very young she was an exhibition dancer, half of a team called Blanco y Negro. Like Dennis at Donohue's and Cathleen at the Sacred Cow, she pours with a golden arm, and you can get yourself happily drunk just watching her move behind the bar. She is also a wit and always good for a laugh. Why some man has not picked her off is hard to say. Sam himself often thought about it.

W. M. Tweed's, like Donohue's, has its complement of cops, though it is not a fuzz joint. When they drink at Donohue's they are supposedly off duty, but when they drink at Tweed's they are definitely on duty, in plainclothes, looking like hippies, watching everybody and listening to everything. Sam recognized some of them, and they pretended not to see him. It really did not matter, for Frankie recognized them too. She said she could smell them.

"Sit at a table," she told Sam when he came in. "I'm going off in a minute."

He took a table and presently she joined him, bringing him a fat Jack Daniel's on the rocks. She started counting her cash.

"How's business?" he said.

"Lousy," she said. "I heard about David. It's a damn shame. How did it happen?"

"We don't know yet," he said. "The cops arrested a junkie, but it wasn't a junkie job."

Well, he thought, it's true, *we* don't know yet. But I know. And if all goes right, Lieutenant Michael Moynihan will soon be Detective Commander Moynihan, a nice rank to retire from.

And better yet, D.C. Gerard Fuseli would become just an unpleasant memory.

Using the bar phone, he called the Castlereagh and told the switchboard operator where he was. There was nothing new, but Jay Murphy, the night man, was on the desk, so Sam got him on the line and asked a few questions about last night's events. Murphy confirmed what Morris Feigl had said: when Saul Braun called the desk around four o'clock to complain about noise coming from Anna Jensen's apartment, they tried to phone the number Sam had left but there was no answer.

"Tell me, Jay," said Sam, "did Anna Jensen call you on the phone around that time—or at any time last night?"

"No, Mr. Kelly, she didn't. I just got this call from Mr. Braun complaining—"

"She didn't call you and ask for help?"

"No, sir."

"'Jay! *Hilf mir! Hilf mir!*' She didn't say something like that?"

"She didn't call me, Mr. Kelly. She didn't call at all."

"All right, Jay. Thanks anyway," Sam said. "By the way, did you know she wasn't Swedish?"

"No, sir."

Well, Sam thought, it figured. Why should old Jay Murphy want to get himself involved in a double murder case? What could there be in it for him? In fact, there *could* be something in it for him. If he gave any useful information to the police—or to Sam Kelly, who was next thing to a cop, from Jay Murphy's viewpoint—the killer might come back and . . . Such a thought was enough, every New Yorker could tell you, to keep otherwise honest citizens from interfering even when they actually saw a murder happening. Jay had not seen it happening. He had, possibly, *heard* it. And this, of course, he would never admit.

"Did you notice any strangers in the lobby around six this morning?" Sam asked.

"You know how it is, Mr. Kelly, strangers coming and going all night long. No, I didn't notice anyone special," Murphy said.

When Sam came back to the table, Frankie was still totting up her afternoon's take. He began to read his newspapers. The *Post* had the bare facts of the double murder, with only a few minor errors. The *News* had the crimes practically solved: a junkie did them. Sam put the papers down, grateful that at least there was nothing in them to scare the real killer off.

He asked Frankie for another Jack Daniel's, and she went back to the bar and poured it for him. Then she got into her cash again.

He sipped slowly, letting his mind empty, hoping for an inspiration. He knew more or less who the killer was. The problem was getting him, bagging him, without getting himself shot. But the problem was not that simple. He also wanted to do something about Fuseli and at the same time do something *for* Mike Moynihan. It was not enough to kill the man who murdered David Christopher.

As he sipped his whiskey he looked casually around the bar. There was a new sign over the backbar, among a profusion of signs with bright sayings like *No Credit*. The new one read:

*Illegitimi non carborundum est!*\*

—J. R. Hoffa

He asked Frankie about James Hoffa's famous bad-Latin saying, and she told him it had been posted over the backbar in commemoration of the recent attempt of a narcotics detective to extort money from the management. A narc had shown the manager a small white glassine package and said it contained heroin and he had found it on the premises. He threatened to get a warrant and toss the whole establishment unless he was paid two hundred dollars. Sam found it hard to believe that any cop could be so stupid, even a narc, but it was a fact. So the manager set this pig up for the bust, and that is the way it went down. It is now a *historical* fact. A large sign was subsequently pasted on the wall, proclaiming this incident to the world. The sign was eventually replaced by the smaller sign over the backbar, Hoffa's advice in Latin bad enough to suit the occasion.

Sam asked Frankie about Raven. Had she heard of this discothéque?

"It's a new one," she said, "over on Second Avenue in the Seventies. I don't know the place. You're not going dancing, are you, Samuel?" She reached across the table and patted his paunch. "But you could use the exercise." She grinned at him. "You're probably just going to ogle the girls, you dirty old man!"

It was now eight fifteen. He decided he would call Madam Bobbie and ask her to go with him

---
\*Don't let the bastards grind you down!

to Raven. It might amuse her.

"Frankie," he said, "do you know the difference between a dirty old man and a dirty young man?"

"Tell me, Daddy."

"Experience!"

He went to the bar phone and dialed Madam Bobbie's number and asked her if she would like to come with him to Raven.

"So you're going to see that wop," she said.

"I'm going to see Devvy," said Sam. "But it's not for the reason you think."

"Well, I don't dance go-go," Madam Bobbie said. "Call me later if your wop girl friend doesn't work out. I'm always available."

She hung up without waiting for his comment, so he went back to the table and asked Frankie for another drink. At half past eight he paid up, said good night to Frankie, and left.

Figuring nine o'clock as being the earliest he might find Devvy Devincenzi at Raven, he took a slow walk up Broadway to 79th Street, where he boarded a crosstown bus. It was nearly nine when he got off the bus at Second Avenue.

**14**

Raven is no more. Discothéques do not live long. Ondine is gone. Together is gone. Youth quickly forgets and takes its pep pills elsewhere. But Raven during its short life was busier than a Honolulu cathouse on Saturday night. It died only a few weeks after the events of our story when a certain Detective Commander Michael Moynihan of Manhattan North raided the premises and arrested the owner-manager on a cocaine and white-slavery rap. It was a nice, clean bust, no goofing, no shooting, and the owner-manager of Raven is presently doing time. He will be doing time for the rest of his unnatural life unless he lives to be a hundred.

Raven took its name from Poe's famous poem, and it was decorated with murals depicting scenes from his poems and stories, "The Fall of the House of Usher," "The Pit and the Pendulum," "The Murders in the Rue Morgue," and so forth. There was also a big blue-black Mexican magpie in a large bamboo cage above the backbar. It was referred to, mistakenly, of course, as The Raven, and it had been taught to croak "Nevermore," which it would do from time to time during the night. Also it shrieked.

Rock music was provided by a group calling itself Pig, whose members wore pink replicas of the New York Police Department uniform but with flaring trousers, wide lapels, and besequined neckties. Also very long hair. Also they came on like fags, but then you cannot be sure with the Hype Generation. During intermissions the management provided a jukebox.

The music was loud and the go-go girls had begun their night's work when Sam came in a little after nine. Like the urraca, they were in cages above the backbar. This kept them out of the customers' reach just in case some drunk wanted to grab a handful. They did their bumps and grinds for twenty minutes at a stretch.

When Devvy saw Sam at the bar she gave him the office, as they say in the criminal underworld, and when she came out of her cage he was waiting for her at the back end of the bar. They took a table and put their heads close together, and he told her a little about the situation at the Castlereagh. All the while he was talking he felt pleasantly aware of her smell, Lanvin's My Sin plus body heat from the heavy go-go dancing.

And then he asked her, "What happened after I saw you in the hotel lobby this morning? You said you were scared. You were going to your apartment. I was going to look in on you later. I did."

"I'm sorry, Sam," she said. "I had to go downtown on an errand. And then I dropped into a movie, and I liked it so much I sat through it twice.

Have you seen *The Godfather?*"

"Yes. What then? I mean, it's been nearly twelve hours since I saw you in the lobby."

"Well, let's see. I went down to the Village and walked around.... Why are you asking, Sam?"

"Mainly," he said, "it's these big black birds. You've seen the one Madam Bobbie has. Did you know that Anna Jensen had one too?"

"No. She's the woman who was killed at the hotel?"

"Yes. And now I find one here too, Devvy."

"I don't understand," she said. "What have these birds got to do with it?"

"Maybe nothing," Sam said. "Maybe everything. Bobbie tells me a man known as Wolfie gave her the one she has."

"I know him," Devvy said.

"You see, it's a very uncommon bird," Sam said. He had heard her, all right, but he needed a moment to think about it. "What about the bird here in this place?"

"Well, the owner imports birds like these—you know, parrots, mynahs..."

Sam said, "He's an exotic-bird importer? Is that his main line?"

"Oh, he's into all kinds of things," Devvy said.

"Does he know Wolfie?"

"Yes."

"How?"

"What do you mean, Sam?"

"How does he know Wolfie?"

"Oh. Well, Bobbie introduced them."

"Did you know this exotic-bird importer before you went to work here?"

"Yes, through Madam Bobbie."

"Of course," Sam said. "How did you happen to take this job, Devvy?"

"I got fed up with tricking. I just got fed up and decided to quit the life."

"I mean," Sam said, "how did you happen to take a job at Raven instead of Macy's or Gimbels?"

"Well, I knew Carlos Luis. He owns this place. Who could live on Macy's wages? Carlos pays good. It's only four hours a night."

"It's hard work," Sam said.

"Tricking isn't?"

Sam studied this flaming redhead for a moment, watching her eyes. In her voice he heard no deception. Now he saw none in her eyes.

"Devvy," he said, "who is Wolfie?"

"A nice man, as they go," she said. "Why?"

"I mean, what does he do for a living? Who is he, really?"

"I don't know," she said. "He always seems to have a lot of money, but I don't know how he gets it. He could be into something with Carlos Luis. . . ."

"What's his right name? Wolfie is just a nickname, isn't it?"

"I don't know, Sam. He was introduced to me as Wolfie, that's all. I don't know where he lives or where he works. I don't even know if he *does* work."

"You said he could be into something with the owner of this place."

"He could be, yes. I don't know. On second thought, I don't think so. He's a very nice man, and Carlos Luis isn't."

"Carlos Luis isn't? What does that mean?"

"Well, people who run places like this,"

she said. "You know . . ."

"I can guess," Sam said. "Girls?"

"Not just that," Devvy said. "Look, Sam, I work for him. I don't want to talk about him."

"Well, Madam Bobbie's in the girl business too," Sam said, "and she's all right."

"Yes. Well, it isn't the same thing, Sam."

He thought that one over. Madam Bobbie and Carlos were both in the girl business, but "it isn't the same thing, Sam." Meaning what? Madam Bobbie got dates for her girls and took her rightful share of the money. What did Carlos Luis do more than that? He used the girls for his own satisfaction? No doubt that was what Devvy meant.

"So Wolfie bought one of these big black birds from Carlos Luis and gave it to Madam Bobbie," said Sam.

"Yes, he gave it to her last Valentine's Day. He taught it to speak a little poem," Devvy said. "We all thought it was pretty cute. Wolfie's a nice old German. Everybody likes him. I think maybe he's retired. Or maybe not. He gives a party now and then, and that's when he calls Madam Bobbie—you know, for girls. And his guests are all well-to-do men like himself. Gentlemen . . ."

"Business associates?"

"Could be."

"So he gives business parties?"

"Could be. I don't know."

"But you've been to his parties?"

"Yes. He always asks for me."

"Does he know you've quit the life?"

"I don't think so. I just took this job the other day. Maybe he knows, if he's talked to Carlos lately —or Madam Bobbie."

"I believe he killed Anna Jensen."

"Sam!"

"I'm sure of it, Devvy."

"Not Wolfie! He wouldn't hurt a fly!"

"So he wouldn't swat a fly. But he'd beat an old woman to death."

"I don't believe it!"

"You will, Devvy. He also killed David Christopher."

"Good God, Sam! David isn't dead?"

"He was killed about two hours after the Jensen woman."

"Sam, I'm scared again!"

"Why should you be? You're not involved, are you?"

"I don't know. Oh, poor David!"

"Is there something you haven't told me, Devvy?"

"Yes. But I don't understand it. I don't know what it means. To think it might have something to do with . . . No! It couldn't!"

"What is it?"

"Now I'm really scared, Sam! Take me out of here! Take me out of this place!"

"All right. Change your clothes and let's go. Where's the dressing room?"

"Back through the curtain. Come with me, I'm afraid to go alone!"

"Lead the way, honey. And be cool. I'm with you."

Devvy got up and started toward the curtain that closed off a hallway at the rear of the big room. A tough-looking character stood by the curtain, or rather in front of it.

"You can't go in there, Jack," he said.

Sam said, "I *am* going in there, Jack. So stand aside."

The toughie started to push Sam back, but Sam suddenly had a small automatic in his hand. So the toughie stepped aside.

The dressing room was down the hallway. Sam waited by the door while Devvy went inside to change. She came out again almost immediately.

"I just put on my street clothes over this go-go costume," she explained. "Come on, let's get out of here!"

As they came through the curtain again the toughie was there, this time holding a gun. And there was someone with him, a short, fat man with a pencil-thin black mustache, brown skin, big sunglasses. He also held a gun.

"Start shooting," Sam said. He still held his own automatic. "You must be Carlos Luis," he said. "I haven't killed anyone today, Carlos, and I need the practice."

The fat Cuban and his toughie stood aside, and Sam and Devvy walked on past them.

Outside they grabbed a Checker cab, and Sam told the cabbie to take them to the Hotel Castlereagh.

## 15

Devvy was laughing. She just lay back in the seat and laughed fit to bust.

"They didn't say a word!" She had to hold her sides, she was laughing so hard. "They're such hard guys!" she said. "And they couldn't *speak!*"

Sam was well pleased. He liked her spirit. She had been afraid, back there at Raven, but now she had recovered her composure and her sense of humor.

Suddenly she flung her arms around him and hugged him tightly. Then she lay back in the seat again and laughed some more, quietly.

"You're not scared now," Sam commented.

"Not now, Sam," she said. "I don't think I'd be scared of anything with you. 'Start shooting!' you said. Oh, wow! That was beautiful!"

"Well, I didn't think they would," Sam said. "But *I* sure as hell would. And I think they knew it."

"You really would?"

"Of course."

"You'd actually kill them?"

"Not necessarily. When you shoot a man with this little automatic of mine, you don't have to kill him. It's a matter of choice. If you want to, you can wound him in such a way that he'll live but he'll think about it for a long time before he tries you again. A shot in the leg or the shoulder is good enough, usually, but if need be you can give him one in the head. Big guns like forty-fives and thirty-eights are for poor souls who need a heavy weapon to make them feel more like a man. Or for cops. When a cop shoots you he wants you definitely down on the ground. Cops are using special slugs in their thirty-eights now, flat-nosed bullets that make a big hole. Something like dumdums. But I'm not a cop, and I'm not a killer, though I can make a citizen's arrest if I want to and I can kill a man if I have to. I'm going to kill the man who murdered David."

"You really believe it's Wolfie?"

"Yes. If I'm wrong, he won't get hurt. But if I'm right, he's a dead man."

"Sam, be careful!"

"I am careful, Devvy."

"But if it's true, if he's killed two people already . . . !"

"Then he'll try to kill me? I agree. But I don't plan to let him do it. You see, he wants something from me. So he won't make the first move. He'll wait until he gets what he wants. That gives me the edge I need."

"You've got it all worked out!"

"All of it. Wolfie is as good as dead right now."

"Why not make a citizen's arrest, like you said? Why kill him?"

"Devvy, he beat an old woman to death, and he shoved a knife in my best friend's back. I don't think a citizen's arrest is good enough."

"Oh, dear, I do hope you're wrong about him. I hope it wasn't Wolfie! He always seemed like such a nice man!"

"Sure, he was a prince. The old woman he beat to death was his wife."

"His wife! Oh, no!"

"They weren't living together. In fact, they weren't even friends anymore, if they had ever been. But that's hardly an excuse for murdering her."

"Why did he do it? Do you know?"

"I'm not sure. I think it was money."

"And David?"

"Why he murdered David? . . . Well, it must have had something to do with the reason he killed his wife. Money. But there's got to be more to it in David's case."

"Sam?"

"Yes?"

"Maybe I can help."

"How."

"Well, with David dead now, I guess I'd better tell you. It's what made me afraid back there at Raven. You said I wasn't in the line of fire, but I'm not so sure. I think I may be. David gave me something to keep for him. It was yesterday afternoon. He came up to my apartment with a dispatch case and asked if he could leave it with me. He said he usually kept it overnight in a safe-deposit box at the bank, but it was after three o'clock, too late for the bank, and could he leave it with me until morning. He said it contained valuable papers, and he was afraid of a robbery. So of course I said yes."

"Where is it, Devvy?"

"Well, I offered to put it in a closet I have with a lock on it, where I keep my own valuables, but he said no, he wanted me to take it down to the desk and have the manager put it in the hotel safe. He said he'd do it himself but he didn't want to be seen carrying it. He said there was no danger for me, only for him. So I did it."

Sam said, "Devvy, I think we've got Wolfie in the bag."

"I saw him in the lobby of the hotel this morning," Devvy said, "just when you were coming in. I wondered what he was doing there."

"Then I must have seen him too," Sam said. "Can you describe him?"

"Tall, thin, distinguished-looking," Devvy said. "Carries a cane."

"And wears a Homburg," said Sam.

"That's him."

"He was wearing gloves too," Sam said. "On a balmy May morning . . . Does he usually?"

"Does he usually what, Sam?"

"Wear gloves."

"I don't think so."

# 16

The hotel lobby was all but empty. At this hour, ten o'clock, the Little Old Ladies and Little Old Men were either asleep in bed or asleep in front of the TV. The hookers were prowling Broadway and Amsterdam Avenue. The horseplayers were doping tomorrow's races. The cops had all gone home. Jay Murphy, the night clerk, was doing the day's transcripts.

Sam asked Murphy to open the safe and take out the dispatch case that Miss Devincenzi had left yesterday afternoon.

Then he and Devvy took it up to his apartment. As he opened the door he observed that someone had used a jimmy and some other tools on it. The locks had not been forced, however, because Sam had personally installed them and nothing less than a battering ram could effect entry once he had locked up. But an attempt had clearly been made.

He did not mention his observation to Devvy, not wanting to alarm her more than she already was.

Baudelaire had come out from his hiding place under the bed and was crouched on the coffee table by the windows, staring at the bird cage.

The big black urraca was perched on the crossbar of his cage, staring at Baudelaire. He had his feathers slightly fluffed, and Baudelaire had his hackles up and his tail doing its Halloween trick.

Devvy was delighted.

"Sam!" she cried. "What have you done to your apartment? So many plants! And such a beautiful cat!" She went to the bird cage. "It's the same kind of bird Madam Bobbie has," she said. "Where did you get it?"

"This one belonged to Anna Jensen," said Sam, "the woman who was murdered last night. The cat was David's. Its name is Baudelaire. And the plants come from David's apartment and from the Jensen woman's. They need washing. See those blood spots?"

"How awful!" Devvy said. "Not David's blood?"

"No," Sam said. "Either Anna Jensen's or the man who murdered her, or both. I suspect both. Wolfie and his Anna. When I get the chance I'll wash the leaves."

"No, I'll do it," Devvy said. "I don't think I could stay in the same room with all that blood!"

She flung her coat onto the couch, went to the kitchen for a sponge and a pot of cold water, and began to wash the blood off Anna Jensen's plants.

With a pocket set of burglar's tools Sam opened the dispatch case. He found two items in it, a typewritten manuscript and a one-hour tape recording. He decided to scan the manuscript first, since this would be the fastest procedure if the pages were a transcript of the tape. By the time he had leafed through the manuscript Devvy had finished washing the leaves of the plants and had gone into the bedroom to shed her go-go costume, which she still wore under her dress. She called to Sam and asked if she might take a shower. He told her to go ahead and make herself at home.

"My house is your house. There's a terry-cloth robe hanging in the bathroom if you want to wear it after."

She went about her showering, and he settled down to give the manuscript a closer scrutiny. The title page read:

WOLFGANG AMADEUS JAEGER
Wall Street Swindler

by Anna Jaeger

The story was familiar—it had all come out in the newspapers. W. A. Jaeger & Company had operated a mutual fund and Jaeger had used the fund to capitalize certain financial ventures of his own. When his manipulations were discovered he had grabbed the negotiable securities and fled to Brazil. The U.S. State Department had started extradition proceedings, and the F.B.I. had begun a search for his ex-wife, Anna Jaeger, who had worked in his office and could therefore be a valuable witness.

Suddenly a few months ago Jaeger had returned from Brazil voluntarily, faced a magistrate, handed over most of the stolen securities, and posted cash bail of one hundred thousand dollars. The F.B.I. still had not found Anna Jaeger.

That was the gist of the Jaeger story as far as Sam and other newspaper readers knew it. But it was enough. Anyone could see why Wolfgang Amadeus Jaeger had decided to return to New York. To silence a potential witness, his wife, Anna Jaeger, alias Anna Jensen. To silence her, yes, but by murder? Was Jaeger's predicament really so serious that he had to kill the chief witness against him? And by beating her to death?

David Christopher's manuscript, bylined by Anna Jaeger, was an inside account of the mutual-fund swindle. It looked as if she wanted to put her ex-husband away, and giving the story to a professional writer was one way of doing it.

So much for the manuscript. Now for the tape recording. Sam took the Chopin études out of his recorder and shoved David Christopher's tape in its place. He expected to hear Anna Jaeger's voice reciting the details of her ex-husband's swindle. But it was David Christopher's voice on the tape, recounting what had been told him by Anna Jaeger. And it had nothing directly to do with the Wall Street swindle.

It was ghostly, hearing David now—David dead, yet speaking clearly, with the perfect diction of a genuinely literary man who had learned his English in maturity. There was the familiar, subtle hint of a foreign origin. You could not have guessed it was Greek, but you knew it was something European—there was something in the value of the vowels. Sam sat stunned, listening as much to the voice as to what it said, perhaps more to the voice than to what it said.

* * *

"I don't know whether this belongs in the book about Jaeger's financial machinations. In any case, I shan't transcribe it until Anna and I have finished writing that manuscript. I do think that perhaps there should be a separate book about Jaeger the Nazi, relating his background in Germany under Hitler, first as a soldier in the *Reichswehr*, then an officer in the S.S., finally a special agent of the Gestapo, and something or other in the United States Office of Strategic Services after the war. None of this came out in the newspaper reports on Jaeger's mutual-fund swindle. I'm getting it by bits and pieces from Anna, late at night, when we are both deep in our cups.

"I can see why she has to talk about it and why she has to get drunk to talk about it. But why talk to *me*, of all people? She has alluded to her own activities as a Nazi. I gather that she played some part in the concentration-camp system, but what exactly she has not yet said. She starts to tell me, and then she veers off onto Jaeger's story again.

"As a soldier in Hitler's army, Jaeger was an expert marksman with the Mauser rifle. He held a non-commissioned officer's rank and was used for sniper work. Later as a commissioned officer in the S.S. he commanded a special assassination squad. By the end of the war he was a Gestapo agent attached to military intelligence and therefore in an excellent position to surrender. He chose to surrender to the U.S. forces, in particular the O.S.S., and he subsequently worked for the O.S.S. until that organization was dissolved. At this point instead of going into the C.I.A. as many O.S.S. men did—and many officers of Hitler's military intelligence—Jaeger went into business on Wall Street as an investment securities consultant and began getting together a mutual fund.

"Clever Nazi that he was, he thought he knew where he was going. Master of his fate. Captain of his soul. Chaucer could have told him six hundred years ago: Radix malorum...."

It was eleven o'clock when Sam finished listening to the tape. If the manuscript supplied a motive for the murders, the tape explained the brutality. A financial swindler might kill to cover his tracks. A Nazi would do so brutally. Well, the police would be glad to get this material. It would be a real coup for Mike Moynihan. No matter that Jaeger would never come to trial.

Yes, and no matter *what*, Jaeger would never come to trial! Of that, Sam thought, David could be sure, wherever he was—adrift in the void, in some Greek limbo...

Then suddenly it struck him like a shot in the head: Jaeger's confidence in returning voluntarily from his Brazilian sanctuary. As a former O.S.S. operative with all that Nazi background, he had connections and he had information. He could blackmail his way out of the swindle rap. He knew he would never come to trial. The dark and secret Powers That Be would descend on the police and on the district attorneys, and Wolfgang Amadeus

Jaeger would get away with murder!

Or he would have gotten away with it, but he made one mistake: he had called Sam Kelly to arrange a deal. Well, he would get a deal, all right. Tomorrow afternoon he would get his deal.

Devvy had showered and put on the terry-cloth robe and afterward sat listening to the tape with Sam.

When it had run its course, she said, "I guess I was wrong about Wolfie when I said he was too nice a man to get into something with Carlos Luis. Let me tell you about Carlos. He's not just in the disco business, as you know, and he's not just in the bird-importing business—anyway, not just Mexican magpies and parrots and mynah birds. He imports another kind of bird: girls from South America and Mexico. Maybe you didn't notice, but most of the girls at Raven are Latins."

"So he's a mac?" Sam said.

"He's one of the biggest macs in the country. He sends girls like me to Rio and Panama and places like that, and he brings their girls up here. It's a circuit. Madam Bobbie works with him. Maybe Wolfie does too. Carlos wanted to get *me* on the circuit. I told him I'd like to dance for a few paydays while I'm thinking it over."

"You wouldn't go for it, would you, Devvy?"

"Are you kidding? I'd probably never get back alive. I'd end up in a crib in Panama City."

"Nice fella, Carlos Luis. Does he have a last name?"

"Carlos Luis Pacheco."

"Do you happen to know what he did in Cuba before the revolution?"

"Before the Cuban revolution? No."

"If he's such a big mac," Sam said, "he's probably into drugs."

"Coke," Devvy said. "That's all I know about. Maybe heroin, but I don't know."

"Girls, birds, and cocaine," Sam said. "Do you know if there's some kind of smuggling connection? I mean, could the girls or the birds be a cover for smuggling the coke?"

"I never thought about it, Sam. I don't know."

"Just a hunch," Sam said.

"Sam!"

"What, Devvy? Something wrong?"

"Do you suppose Wolfie knows about these things that David gave me to keep for him?"

"Definitely, yes."

"Then maybe he knows *I've* got them!"

"I doubt it."

"But we don't *know*, Sam!"

"True."

"Sam, I'm scared again! Can I stay here with you? I mean, just for tonight?"

"Of course. Bedroom or parlor couch?"

"The couch is fine. Thanks, Sam. If there's anything I can do for you . . ."

"You don't have to do anything for me, Devvy. Did you want to go to bed now?"

"Whenever you turn in. I'm used to late hours."

"Well, I thought I'd try for a long night's sleep," Sam said. "I've got a heavy day tomorrow."

"Okay by me. Whenever you say."

"Would you care for a little something first?"

"Like what?"

"Jack Daniel's, Rémy Martin, a bottle of Beck's . . . ?"

"What I'd *really* like, Sam . . ."
"Tell me, Devvy."
"Would you believe hot chocolate?"

# 17

"Right on!" Sam said. "I'll prepare it for you."

"I can do it," Devvy said.

"Good, then. Fix yourself a hot chocolate. I'll have some Rémy Martin."

While Devvy got her hot chocolate ready, Sam put a tape of *The Art of the Fugue* on the recorder and then poured himself a big, fat cognac. Straight, no rocks. Then he sat back in a big easy chair by the window and watched the night. It was clear and for once you could see stars in the New York sky. You could also see Madam Bobbie's windows directly across the way. They were lighted up. He felt a pang of regret, and he had to remind himself that she was in business with Carlos Luis Pacheco and probably with Jaeger too. She knew more than she had admitted to, and this could be dangerous. Or could have been. It was nearly over now, and he was calling the shots.

The pun was unintentional, of course, but it made him smile.

"What's funny?" Devvy asked as she came back to the parlor with her hot chocolate.

"It's a night for puns," Sam said. "You and your hot chocolate!"

"I meant it, Sam. I really dig you."

"I'm pleased, Devvy."

"But you have a thing going with Madam Bobbie, haven't you?"

"I had," Sam said. "What I've learned tonight changes that. Tonight and this afternoon. She hasn't been leveling with me. It could be dangerous, or it could have been. But let's not talk about that." He finished his cognac. "Well," he said, "good night, Devvy."

He went into the bedroom and undressed, hung up his clothes, and got into bed.

Devvy called to him, "Sam?"

"Just pull back the couch cover," he said. "The bed's already made up."

"Sam?"

"Yes?"

"May I sleep with you?"

## 18

The phone rang at nine A.M. Sam raised up on one elbow, fumbled with the receiver, and said hello. It was the desk. Mr. Singh had two special-delivery letters for Mr. Kelly. They had just arrived. Should he bring them up? Sam thought about it.

"Yes," he said. "Give me five minutes."

In precisely five minutes Mr. Singh knocked at the door. Sam leaped out of bed. The Pakistani gave him the two envelopes. Sam thanked him and went back to the bedroom. The envelopes had no return address. He had not expected any.

Devvy was watching him as he came into the bedroom.

"Good news?" she asked.

"Money," he said as he opened the envelopes. He shook out their contents, letting the bills fall and scatter over her. "Lettuce for breakfast!"

She laughed and clutched bunches of the bills and tossed them up in the air.

"I've never seen so much money, Sam!" she cried.

She opened her arms to him as he climbed back into bed.

The phone rang again in a little while. Sam looked at the clock. Nine thirty. Too early. He reached across Devvy and switched it off. Now the fool thing could ring its little heart out in silence.

Later, at five to ten, he reached out again and switched it on, and presently it rang. This time he answered it.

"Hello. Schmidt?"

"Yes, Mr. Kelly. Did my special-delivery envelopes arrive yet?"

"Yes, Mr. Schmidt. And I have good news for you."

"I was sure you would have. Now I will tell you how to send the material to me. Write this address—"

"No, Mr. Schmidt," said Sam. "I am going to give you the material personally. But first let us discuss the terms."

"Terms, Mr. Kelly?"

"Fifty thousand dollars in cash, used bills, nothing larger than a twenty."

"That's a lot of money. You already have five thousand."

"That's only my retainer. We agreed on that."

"Yes, we did. But still, fifty thousand . . ."

"I could get that much from somebody else, Mr. Schmidt."

"Very well. You have me at a disadvantage. I agree. Fifty thousand dollars. How shall we make the exchange?"

"At Lincoln Center in the plaza by the fountain at exactly three o'clock this afternoon. Do not come early, and do not be late, or the deal is off."

"Will you describe the material to me, Mr. Kelly?"

"A typewritten manuscript and a tape recording. One manuscript and one recording."

"Have you examined the manuscript and the tape?"

"I have, Mr. Schmidt. They are what you want."

"Good! But there yet remains one problem. How are we going to check each other's packets, you the money and I the manuscript and tape?"

"After we meet, we will go to a hotel. I will reserve a suite. I will also bring a tape recorder with me. You will examine the manuscript and audition the tape while I count the money. Agreed?"

"Except for one thing. Have you read the document or listened to the tape?"

"Of course, Mr. Schmidt."

"I wonder, Mr. Kelly. Do you really have these things in your possession?"

"Of course."

"But I wonder. I suspect you are not being entirely honest with me."

"Why do you say that?"

"Because, Mr. Kelly, you are still addressing me as Mr. Schmidt."

"Very shrewd," Sam said. "Shall I address you as Herr Jaeger?"

"Thank you, Mr. Kelly. Three o'clock, then, by the fountain in the plaza at Lincoln Center. It is indeed a pleasure doing business with you, sir."

Sam hung up the phone wondering at Jaeger's apparent composure. How could the man feel so sure? Did the damned Nazi have a trump card up his sleeve? He had sure as hell had one at the end of World War II when he finagled his own surrender to the O.S.S. and saved his rotten hide from the Nuremburg trials and a hangman's rope.

Devvy had been listening, of course, but she had heard only Sam's end of the conversation.

"Fifty thousand dollars!" she exclaimed.

"That's probably just talk," Sam said. "I don't really expect him to bring the money. When we get to the hotel he plans to rip me off. Only we're not going to a hotel. The whole deal goes down right there by the fountain."

"You're selling him the manuscript and the tape?"

"No. Of course not."

"Then you're ripping *him* off?"

"Right."

"Is there anything I can do to help?"

"Can you cook?"

"How's that?"

"Breakfast."

"I thought you'd never ask."

"I'll shave while you're cooking."

Devvy kissed him and bounced out of bed with the morning energy of her twenty-three years. She pulled on the terry-cloth robe and went to the kitchen.

Sam eased himself out of bed and went into the bathroom. The thought of a home-cooked breakfast prepared by gentler hands than his was giving him a ravenous appetite. As he lathered up he wondered what Devvy would do now that she had quit the hustle. She had certainly lost her job at Raven. He stropped the razor a few strokes, then touched it to his cheek and drew it down. Smooth. Like stroking a baby's bottom. He could smell sausage broiling.

"How do you like your eggs?" Devvy called to him.

"Sunny side up!" he called back.

"Okay! Ten minutes to breakfast!"

Funny how Madam Bobbie had never cooked for him, he thought as he washed and dried the blade. She simply did not cook, neither breakfast nor lunch nor dinner, though she claimed she could. She kept delicatessen stuff in her refrigerator, canned foods in the kitchen cabinets, nothing that was not already prepared. Even the coffee and the tea were instant. If he said he was hungry, she suggested they go to Tweed's for a hamburger, to Casa Delmonte for lasagna, to La Crêpe for crepes. Or she would phone the Gingko Tree for egg rolls and chow mein or Stampler's for a ready-cooked steak dinner.

The rich aroma of percolating Colombian coffee drifted in from the kitchen. The phone rang. It was Lieutenant Moynihan.

"We finally got Anna Jensen's fingerprints identified," he said.

"Anna Jaeger," said Sam, "alias Anna Jensen."

"How in hell did you know that?"

"Us private eyes have our little secrets, Mike. What else is new?"

"Maybe *you* could tell *me*, shamus!"

"Don't get hard, Mike. Let's be friends. Are you still holding Rodney, the junkie punk?"

"He was released an hour ago. The D.C. now has a theory that Anna Jaeger's husband killed her. The F.B.I. wants her as a witness in Jaeger's stock swindle. That's motive. He wanted to silence her. But it doesn't explain why he killed your friend David Christopher."

"Sure it does. The woman was giving information to David, and he was writing it up for publication. Jaeger knew this."

"So Christopher could have testified against him too."

"Right."

"You can prove this?"

"I can. And I will."

"I'd better come to your place. We have to talk, Sam. I want everything you've got."

"And I'm going to give it to you, Mike, the whole megillah. But not here. Don't you come anywhere near this hotel. We'll meet at O'Neals' Baloon at two thirty this afternoon."

"It's only ten thirty now. Can't you make it sooner?"

"No," Sam said. "Trust me, Mike. I'm going to give you this case wrapped as a gift, but you have to let me do it my way. Two thirty at O'Neals' Baloon. Do you know the place?"

"You said Baloon? There's an O'Neals' over on Columbus by Seventy-second."

"Same owner, different location. The Baloon occupies the northwest corner of the Empire, which is a hotel across the avenue from Lincoln Center."

"Okay. Two thirty."

"And bring Detective Commander Fuseli and enough men to handle Jaeger."

"What? Don't kid a kidder, boy!"

"Thanks for the *boy*, Mike."

"Sorry, Sam. It just slipped out. You were saying?"

"I'm giving you Jaeger at three o'clock sharp."

"For God's sake, Sam, we need more lead time!"

"Not you, Mike. You could take him alone any

time. But you'll have the D.C. with you, so you'd better make sure you have a couple of men to cover for *him*."

"Watch it, Sam! I'm phoning from the precinct!"

"Good! Maybe Fuseli's listening."

"Just take it easy, will you, boy?" Moynihan gulped so loud you could hear it. "Sorry, Sam."

"See you at two thirty," Sam said. "And when you *boys* come into O'Neals', try not to look like cops, will you? And don't walk in all together like a squad on parade. Come in singly. I'll have a booth at the back by the east wall. Don't be late."

He hung up.

Not having had supper last night, he felt uncommonly hungry now.

## 19

It was a little after eleven when they finished breakfast. Sam drank the last of his coffee, with heavy cream, dabbed his lips with his napkin, and sighed profoundly.

"Baby, you can really burn!"

"Just a simple breakfast, Sam. You should try my eggs Devincenzi."

"How's that?"

"Poached in cream gravy, served on slabs of spoon bread—"

"Enough, girl! Enough! Have mercy!"

"Do you like hushpuppies?"

"Get out of town—!"

"With little bits of smoked ham in the puppies?"

"—before it's too late!"

"And corn fritters?"

"I'll marry you!"

"Hocks and butter beans? Collards?"

"I'll marry you twice! Where do you hail from, child? How come Maria Devincenzi talks Southern cooking like a native?"

"I'm from Tennessee, sir, a little place outside Nashville, but I was born on the Lower East Side. My father is an honest tailor, and he bought a small business through *The New York Times* and moved us, poor Mother and me, down South when I was just a little, tiny baby. Do you want to hear my life story, sir?"

"I do indeed, ma'am," said Sam.

"Thank you, sir. It's the sad, sad story of a naturally unlucky broad. In high school I starred in the senior play, a piece called *Smilin' Through,* and I did the Norma Shearer part. This aroused my interest in theater. Talk about unlucky! It couldn't be chemistry or nursing or anything sensible like that. Theater! So I decided to come to New York and go on the stage. That was five years ago. I made the rounds of the agencies and got nowhere. I still make the rounds and get nowhere. I couldn't hold a regular job and see the agents every day, so I sort of drifted into hustling. What a dumb story!"

"Then you're an actress," Sam said. "I often wondered. Strange that David never mentioned it. Did he know?"

"Yes. Did he tell you he got me off the street? He sent me to Madam Bobbie."

"I know," Sam said. "So what are you going to do now? You blew the gig at Raven last night."

"I guess I could give Madam Bobbie a call. She'd probably take me back."

"Is that what you want to do?"

"No."

"Discothéque?"

"Ugh!"

"Maybe I've got a plan for you."

"Think so?"

"Interested?"

"We could talk about it."

"We'll talk about it over lunch."

"But we just had breakfast, Sam!"

"We'll be hungry by the time we get to it, Devvy. We're lunching at O'Neals' Baloon."

"Goodie! Can I watch you capture Wolfie?"

"You'll have a ringside seat, honey. Shall we shower now? Or would you prefer a tub?"

"Shower, if this creepy hotel doesn't run out of hot water in the middle of everything. Are we taking our shower together?"

"Is there another way?"

They took a long, long shower and scrubbed one another very, very clean, and the hotel's boilers held up nicely to the end. It was high noon by the time they had toweled each other dry. Sam suggested they lounge around awhile with a couple of drinks.

"We have a little time to kill," he said. "Do you like bourbon?"

"Am I from Tennessee?"

"Well, Devvy, if you can make drinks like you cook . . ."

"How do you take your bourbon, Sam?"

"On the rocks."

"You wouldn't happen to have some hothouse mint and an ice shaver?"

"Mint juleps! Chile, dem is de fustes' victuals we gone buy, me an' you, when we sets up housekeepin': fresh mint an' a ice shavuh! An' we gone live on mint juleps an' ham hocks an' buttah beans an' collahd greens an' corn fritters an' yams an' cream gravy an' spoon bread. We gone eat ourselfs into a happy grave!"

"Sam! You forgot hushpuppies!"

"God bless hushpuppies!"

Devvy walked naked into the kitchen and got the bourbon and the ice cubes and glasses together, and she brought two Jack Daniel's on the rocks into the bedroom.

"Devvy, honey," Sam said, "do you happen to own a picture hat?"

"Why, Sam! You're a romantic!"

"I am?"

"Picture hats!"

"Oh."

"I'll wear something slinky with it, shall I? And French heels? And a feather boa?"

"Some cowards hide behind a woman's dress," Sam said. "Not this one. I'm a romantic. I'm going to hide behind your picture hat."

"What?"

"It's called thinking ahead, honey, and you'll see when we get to O'Neals' Baloon."

## 20

By one thirty they had had two more big Jack Daniel's and an early matinee *and* were ready to go out. Sam gathered up the five thousand dollars in small bills, made a neat package, and gave it to Devvy to hold for him. She put it in her purse.

"Just in case anything should happen to me," he told her.

"You don't think anything will, Sam!"

"Nothing will, Devvy. But just in case . . ."

"Be careful, love," she said. "I don't want to lose you now."

He thought that over as he put the tape recording and the manuscript in the black dispatch case.

When they were in the hallway, he smelled the fragrance of marijuana smoke again but decided to let it wait. He felt much too pleased with life to bother Angela Grandville, whoever she was, and her tall, dark girl friend about a trivial thing like smoke. Also he did not feel like phoning Madam Bobbie at the moment. He would do it later, maybe tomorrow, and ask her to tell her two new girls not to make their reefer smoking quite so public. Meanwhile, *absit trivia*.

On the way to the lobby they stopped by Devvy's apartment for her to change into something slinky and to get her picture hat.

The place had been tossed as thoroughly as Anna Jaeger's or David Christopher's, but there was no sign of the door having been forced.

"Did you double-lock the door when you left?" Sam asked. "Either the intruder had a key or he slipped the lock with a strip of celluloid."

"I don't remember, Sam. I do sometimes forget to double-lock."

"Well, it's a good thing you didn't stay here last night, honey."

"In more ways than one," Devvy said.

Sam took her hand and kissed it. "Thank you, Devvy."

"My pleasure, sir!"

"I'll help you put this place together again after lunch," Sam said. "Right now I think we'd best move on. So don your slinky dress and the French heels and the picture hat, and let's go."

While she changed, he phoned O'Neals' Baloon and reserved the table he wanted in the back corner by the east wall. This location would enable him to observe the front dining area, the bar, the glassed-in sidewalk café, and Lincoln Center plaza all at the same time.

He told the maître d', whose name was Alex, "I'd like you to have the bartender prepare mint juleps. Four should be enough. If Tom is on duty, tell him they're for Sam Kelly."

There was nothing new in the lobby when they

got downstairs. Little Morris Feigl was standing by the desk. Mr. Singh, the day clerk, was standing behind it. Sam told them he would be out until three thirty or later having lunch at O'Neals' Baloon. He did not want to be called unless there was an earthquake or a revolution.

Feigl glanced at Devvy and said to Sam, "Enjoy! Enjoy!"

Sam thanked him, smiling on the world. At the moment there were no shady characters around. They would be out mugging citizens, ripping off apartments, soliciting on the street, trying to pass bad checks, shoplifting, anything that came to hand. And the Little Old Ladies and Little Old Men were either having lunch or getting ready for their afternoon nap. The horseplayers were of course up at the O.T.B. on 72nd Street taking care of business. Sam remembered that he had a ten-dollar ticket in his wallet, Sweetie Pie on the nose in the seventh at Belmont yesterday. He would have to check the results.

Saturday the sixth of May was as promising a day as Friday the fifth had been. The time-and-temperature sign on the southern face of the massive Central Savings Bank said 1:45 and 74 degrees. The air was balmy as Sam and Devvy came out of the hotel. A sweet zephyr rustled the young leaves of the trees in Verdi Square, and traffic was light along Broadway.

"Shall we cab it?" Sam asked.

"Let's walk," Devvy said.

She took his arm and they strolled along the broad sidewalk in the early afternoon sun, lazy as lizards, contented as cats.

They passed a White Rose and the rich, beery

smell beckoned them, but they walked on by. Russians in a Chekhov film greeted them from the two-sheets as they passed the lobby of the Regency Theatre. Across Broadway the Cinema Studio offered a brace of old James Bond flicks. Checker cabs and limousines were running up the Lincoln Center ramp in a steady flow, letting well-dressed gentry out for an afternoon of ballet.

Devvy said, "Look, Sam! Madam Bobbie!"

Sam looked and saw her riding down Broadway in a taxi, wearing the same outfit he had enjoyed yesterday when they went to the Fleur de Lis: stiffly starched high-necked white blouse with much lace at the neck, blue fox stole with pink-dyed mink lining, all red, white, and blue.

"I always feel patriotic when I see her," Sam said. He felt slightly disloyal saying it to one of her former girls. "It's the red, white, and blue," he explained.

"I know," Devvy said. "The girls call her Old Glory." She squeezed his arm. "For God's sake, don't tell her, Sam!"

"Well, I doubt if Bobbie and I will be having any long dialogues, Devvy," he said. "Something's wrong. I don't know what it is. But I don't trust her now."

"Care to talk about it?"

"I don't think so. I can tell you one thing, though. She hasn't really leveled with me. But I don't think I want to talk about it."

It was not just the fact that she had turned off the telephone so that he hadn't got his call from the hotel. Had he got that call, David might be alive now. But then, he had to admit, this could have been coincidence, the breaks, the luck. And it was not just the fact that she had checked a couple of new girls into the Castlereagh without telling him. Surely there was nothing in that. No, something else was bothering him. He would probably never know the truth, but he had to consider the possibility that the urraca he had heard screeching over the telephone when he was talking with Richard Schmidt—the lovable character known as Wolfie and now identified as Wolfgang Amadeus Jaeger—was Bobbie's own big black Mexican magpie, and that Jaeger had called from her apartment in the Charmian Towers.

He didn't know this, couldn't prove it, and didn't really want to. But the suspicion was there, and it brought up other thoughts. Her profession, for instance. He despised pimps, and whenever he could do one of them a hurt he did it. But he had always looked the other way where Madam Bobbie was concerned. The girls themselves he understood and felt sympathy for. But those who lived off them . . . Everything considered, he didn't think that he and Madam Bobbie would have quite the same relationship now, if any at all.

The glassed-in sidewalk café of O'Neals' Baloon was full of modish young persons eating and drinking.

Alex, the maitre d', had Sam's table ready. It was in the back corner by the east wall, as he had requested. From here he could see without being seen. He could observe not only this whole section of the Baloon *and* the street door, but also Lincoln Center plaza across Columbus Avenue.

"I want you to sit with your back to the entrance," he told Devvy. "Your picture hat will conceal both of us if Jaeger decides to come in. He might. He's sure to check out the situation around the fountain before three o'clock. He could study the scene from the bar here, or from one of the Lincoln Center windows, say, Philharmonic Hall, or even from the Empire upstairs, or almost anywhere —with binoculars from that big high-rise over on Central Park West—but if he comes *here* your hat hides me. It's five after two now."

Devvy said, "So that's what you meant by thinking ahead. And I thought you were a romantic!"

The waiter brought them two mint juleps, fresh from the freezer. Glancing around Devvy's big hat, Sam could see Tom at the bar. Sam recalled how Tom used to call him and David the Jack Daniel's twins, Jack and Daniel, and always served their J.D.'s on the rocks in Manhattan glasses.

Sam told the waiter, "A dozen raw cherrystones for me, please." And to Devvy: "How about you, honey?"

She said yes and began to study the menu as she sipped her julep.

After a moment she said, "It's a good julep, Sam. But I do it better. The barman used a sour mash."

"That's because he knew the juleps were for me," Sam said.

"Sweet bourbon is better for juleps," Devvy said.

"I prefer sour mash," Sam said.

"Too heavy for juleps," Devvy said. "Sour mash is for sipping, sweet for mixing, and don't contradict me. I'm from Tennessee, remember."

Sam was keeping an eye on the street door, peering carefully around the wide brim of Devvy's picture hat. At twenty-five after two Lieutenant Moynihan walked in. He stood at the door a moment, looking the place over. Sam waved to him and he came to the table and sat down.

While Sam was introducing him to Devvy another man came in. He was the Homburg-hatted, Windsor-cravatted gentleman that Sam had observed yesterday morning in the lobby of the Hotel Castlereagh. He had taken this elegant gent for an unemployed actor of the older generation, or even a writer or singing teacher. Now he took him for Wolfgang Amadeus Jaeger, the well-known Wolfie. And he observed that the man still wore the strip of adhesive plaster on his left cheek and that he still wore gloves.

Jaeger looked about and possibly saw Devvy's big picture hat, but he could not see her face and he could not see Sam. He carried a black dispatch case and a cane. The cane had a pistol grip. He went directly to the bar and sat where he could look through the many windows of the glassed-in sidewalk café and across Columbus Avenue to the Lincoln Center plaza and the fountain. He did not take off his gloves. And he sat with his back to the street door and the dining area.

Sam saw Tom draw a beer and put it in front of Jaeger. He watched the man sip it, and he wondered where exactly in his back to place the bullet. Just under the left shoulder blade? Jaeger had stabbed David there. But if he went for the heart, a rib might deflect the bullet and he would miss the kill. No, he would have to make sure. A shot in the backbone would make certain.

Another man came in then. Sam figured him for a cop. He saw Moynihan and headed straight back to Sam's table. Detective Commander Fuseli entered next. When he sat down, the whole detail was present except for the two plainclothes backup men in the front seat of a black Ford that could be seen standing in the bus stop by the little park opposite the Lincoln Center plaza.

"I take it we're all here," Sam said after he had completed the introductions. "I'm going to give you Wolfgang Amadeus Jaeger, the Wall Street swindler and murder of his ex-wife and of my good friend. At three o'clock I will deliver Jaeger and the evidence."

"We were already on to him," Detective Commander Fuseli said. "But it's a circumstantial case. He had motive, but we can't prove he did it. You *can?*"

"Yes."

"Material evidence?"

"A manuscript and a tape recording."

"And you say you're turning this material over to us at three o'clock? Why not now?"

"Because I want to give you Jaeger, red-handed, at the same time. The whole megillah goes as a package, Commander, at three o'clock sharp, in the Lincoln Center plaza, by the fountain. Jaeger will bring fifty thousand dollars in cash. He will be expecting me to sell him the evidence you want. At this point you will make the arrest."

"So you have it all set up," Fuseli said. "But I need to know more, Kelly. How did you get hold of the evidence?"

"That is privileged information, Commander," said Sam. "As a private investigator I don't have to reveal my sources. All I have to do is give you the evidence, not tell you how I got it."

"But we could be walking into a trap!" Fuseli said. "Why should we trust *you?*"

Sam said, "I remember when you walked into

one, Commander. You set up your deal so well I got shot in the foot and a young cop named Coogan got his brains blown out. So you take your chances with *me* this time, Commander, or you don't. Who needs you, anyway?"

"Kelly, you son of a bitch!" Fuseli said.

The D.C.'s face was apoplectic red. Sam could see that Moynihan was amused. The other cop just stared at the tablecloth.

"A couple of minutes before three," Sam said, "I'll leave here and walk straight to the fountain. Jaeger won't be far behind me."

"How do you know this?" Fuseli demanded. "How can you be sure he'll be on time?"

"He's already here," Sam said.

"Where?"

"Never mind. Now, as I said, he'll be right behind me on the march across the plaza. You'll probably make him when you see him following me. In any case, I want you following him but not too close. You will see us open our dispatch cases. That's when you move. You will have to move fast. But be careful. He has already murdered two people."

Fuseli said, "All right, Kelly. We'll go along. But you'd better be right. You say you have material evidence, something Jaeger wants, and that provides motive. It still doesn't prove he killed anyone."

Sam said, "I can place him at the scene of the crime."

"You do that, Kelly, and I will personally apologize for what I think of you," Fuseli said.

"Commander, I wouldn't want you to change your opinion of me," Sam said. "As it is, I feel like the farmer who got kicked by the mule: I just consider the source."

"You bastard, Kelly!"

"Hush, Commander. Lady present."

"Kelly, by Christ—!"

"Cool it, Commander! And listen. I'm going to give you an elementary lesson in the detective art of observation. Do you recall seeing a motion-picture camera crew on the traffic island in the middle of Broadway yesterday morning?"

"So?"

"Well, I'm fairly sure you'll find Jaeger in some of the footage."

"Fairly sure? Not good enough, Kelly!"

"Not good enough for *you*, Commander? How come? I remember when you would walk right into a trap with perfect self-confidence."

"Enough of that, Kelly."

"If necessary, Commander, *I* can identify him for you. I have seen Jaeger."

"Where? When?"

"In the lobby of the Hotel Castlereagh yesterday morning around nine forty-five."

"Now, what would Jaeger be doing there four hours after the second murder? Kelly, you've been smoking something."

"I don't know what he was doing there," Sam said. "And it doesn't matter. Maybe he was eavesdropping on the cops. I'd put money on it. But in any case, he was there. I'm sure the movie people got him when he left. He's a very distinguished-looking type, and those movie cameramen were making pick-up shots. They wouldn't be likely to miss him."

Commander Fuseli stared hard at Sam, very

skeptically, and finally said to Moynihan, "Go out to the car, Lieutenant, and explain the procedure to the back-up men. Stay with them and take charge of them when the action starts. I'll take Jaeger myself. Just be sure you're behind me when I make my move."

"Yes, sir," Moynihan said.

He left. It was five minutes to three.

"Maybe you better get started," Fuseli said to Sam.

"Not quite yet," Sam said. "I'll call the shots, Commander." And to Devvy he said, "Wait for me here, honey. I should be back in ten minutes." Leaning close to her and whispering in her ear, he said, "Don't look now, but Wolfie is at the bar. He hasn't seen us, so don't worry. He wouldn't try anything in here. I figure he'll leave the bar as soon as he sees me on the sidewalk. Then you can move to this side of the table and watch the action. Meanwhile, be very careful how you peek around the brim of that big hat."

He got up and took her hand and kissed it.

"*You* be careful, Sam!" she said.

He headed for the street door, carrying the black dispatch case. Jaeger would not see him until he got outside and passed along the windows of the glassed-in sidewalk café.

When he hit the street he did not look back. A bit of calculated risk, that. Jaeger just might sneak up behind him, shoot him, grab the dispatch case, and climb into a waiting car. But Sam didn't think so. Jaeger would want to be very certain that the dispatch case actually contained the manuscript and the tape recording.

The light at the pedestrian crossing went red and

Sam had to wait. Standing at the crossing, he had the creepy, hair-raising feeling that Jaeger had already left the bar and was close behind him. He glanced uptown and out of the corner of his eye he saw the man not three paces behind, dispatch case in one hand, cane in the other. The light turned green.

Sam started to cross the avenue, trying to maintain a normal pace. He heard the sharp rapping of hard leather heels close behind.

He climbed the steps to the plaza level and continued straight across the open space to the fountain. The waterworks were turned on full and their mechanism was changing the water patterns. The cascading waters splintered the sunlight a thousand ways, and there was a little breeze blowing, enough to waft a fine spray and create a lovely rainbow.

Sam opened the button of his jacket so he could reach his pistol pocket more easily. There were a few children walking around the raised rim of the fountain's pool. Some long-haired youths were sitting about. A group of tourists were pointing cameras at the fountain. Well, they were going to get some fine souvenir snapshots, all right, Sam thought, memories of Little Old New York.

He turned and faced Jaeger. Over the man's shoulder he saw Detective Commander Fuseli coming up fast, with Moynihan and the back-up men behind him.

Jaeger said, "Well, Mr. Kelly, shall we go? You have reserved a hotel room?"

Sam said, "Have you brought the money?"

Jaeger snapped open his case, displaying many green bundles of tens and twenties.

Sam opened his, showing the manuscript and the tape recording.

Commander Fuseli was close enough now. He stopped and drew his gun. He held his badge ready to show. Moynihan and the others flanked him.

Jaeger must have seen that Sam was watching something behind him. Perhaps he actually saw a reflection in Sam's eyes. Suddenly he understood.

"The money wasn't enough?" he said quietly.

Sam didn't answer him.

Commander Fuseli said, very loudly, "Jaeger, you're under arrest! Police Department! Don't move!"

But Jaeger moved very fast. He dropped his dispatch case, gripped the cane in both hands, turned as he raised it to belt level, and pointed it at Fuseli's gut.

The D.C. stared at him, not recognizing the cane for what it really was.

Sam had whipped his own gun out of his pistol pocket as soon as Jaeger turned to face Fuseli, and now he jammed it hard against the man's back and cocked the hammer.

"One shot and you're dead, Jaeger!"

But Jaeger cranked off his one shot, catching Fuseli just above the belt buckle, dead center. Fuseli fell backward as if a cannonball had knocked him over. Citizens around the fountain scattered like startled pigeons.

Sam pulled the trigger of his little automatic just once, blasting away a section of Jaeger's backbone, killing him instantly.

Lieutenant Moynihan and the back-up men were firing as Jaeger fell, and they were all close enough to score. But they were scoring off a dead man. Sam had the deep satisfaction of knowing that his own little .25-caliber bullet had done the job.

Now that the shooting was over, security guards came running out of Philharmonic Hall and out of the New York State Theater and other buildings, and a crowd began to close in. Lieutenant Moynihan told the guards to keep the people back.

An ambulance came howling around the corner of Broadway from in front of the Hotel Empire, where it had been waiting on Detective Moynihan's orders. Moynihan examined the D.C. He was in shock and dying fast. Most of his blood was on the pavement of the plaza.

Sam picked up the cane and looked it over. It had a 410-gauge bore. Probably loaded with buckshot rather than birdshot, he judged, and backed by an extra-heavy load of powder.

Kneeling by Jaeger's body, Sam ripped the adhesive plaster off the dead man's face. As he had suspected, Jaeger had not cut himself shaving. The cut was deep, not the accidental kind. Anna Jaeger had got in at least one good lick before the end. Sam peeled off one of Jaeger's gloves. More cuts. This would have happened while he was trying to disarm his wife. Then he had beaten her to death. And while she was unconscious, if not already dead, he had cut her throat.

Moynihan had been watching Sam, and now he said, "The woman must have fought hard. This explains the two blood types in her room."

Sam said, "It also explains why David was killed two hours later. It took Jaeger that long to patch himself up. He must have been bleeding heavily."

"But how did he get into your friend's apartment?" Moynihan asked. "Did Anna Jaeger have a key?"

"Possibly," Sam said. "Or maybe David got so drunk he forgot to double-lock his door when he came in. I would imagine Jaeger knew how to slip a plain lock with a piece of stiff celluloid."

Indeed, he had no doubt of it. Someone had done exactly that to Devvy's door. It had to have been Jaeger. But Sam did not tell this to Moynihan. Much as he liked and trusted the big mick, he didn't want to involve Devvy.

By the time the ambulance attendants had put Fuseli in the ambulance he was dead. They loaded Jaeger in the meat wagon with him and headed downtown to the city morgue, slowly—no need for sirens, no need to hurry now, for Jaeger and Fuseli, the two masterminds, had already arrived at their common destination.

Sam gave Moynihan the two dispatch cases containing tape, manuscript, and money.

"You've done a fine job today, Commander," he said.

"What commander?" said Moynihan. "This is no time for jokes!"

"Lieutenant, you'll be Detective Commander Moynihan before you're a week older," Sam said.

"Sam, don't talk nonsense!"

"Mike, you've solved the murders at the Castlereagh, you've got the evidence, and you've caught the man you were after when even the F.B.I.—"

"Sam! If I thought you set this up . . ."

"We'll celebrate your coming promotion, shall

we? How about having lunch with Miss Devincenzi and me? I'm buying."

"Lunch? You've got to come to the precinct. There's a report to be made, your testimony . . ."

"Keep me out of it, Mike. Play it like I said. *You* solved the case. Maybe I helped a little. You'll retire next year as detective commander. Okay?"

"Sam, Sam . . ."

"This is your chance, Mike."

"But why are you doing this?" Moynihan asked. "You got the evidence together, you set up the arrest—even if it didn't go off right. Sam! Damn it, Sam, if what I'm thinking—"

"Case closed, Mike."

The big man looked away, back toward O'Neals' Baloon, and took a deep breath. He sighed.

"Call me at the precinct after you and your lady friend finish lunch," he said. "There might be something . . ."

"I'll do that."

Although the cops and the guards had pretty well dispersed the crowd of onlookers, quite a scattering of people still hung around, standing well back from Lieutenant Moynihan and Sam, watching them and staring at the place where the shoot-out had just taken place. The blood had not yet been mopped up. It shone bright scarlet in the spring sunshine.

As Sam walked back to O'Neals' Baloon the people stepped aside to let him pass, though they hadn't been standing close together. They seemed to want to give him plenty of room. Not that any of them had seen him shoot Jaeger in the spine. That wasn't likely. But he had been somehow part of the violence, and he carried it with him.

As he crossed Columbus Avenue he saw that the faces inside the glassed-in sidewalk café were turned toward the plaza, and that some were staring at him. He did not answer their stare. He began to wonder if it might not be better to take Devvy somewhere else for lunch.

More people were crowded around the entrance to the Baloon, gawking. Alex, the maître d', had seen Sam coming, however, and he cleared the entrance for him. Then he personally escorted Sam back to his table. Every eye in the restaurant was turned toward them, toward the amiable-looking dark-skinned man and his glamorous red-haired woman in the great picture hat.

"Alex," said Sam, "I don't think I enjoy being a celebrity. Have you got a screen to put around the table?"

"Yes, Mr. Kelly," said Alex. "I'll bring it right away."

He left to do so. Sam sat down. He and Devvy were sitting at the same side of the table now, and she kissed him on the cheek.

"My hero!" she said.

"Moynihan is the hero today," Sam said. "I didn't even get to keep the fifty grand. It's evidence." He remembered to take off his yellow straw boater and hang it on a wall hook. He ran his hand over his bald pate and found he had been sweating a little, just a little. He wondered if the shoot-out would catch up with him later. He thought it probably would. An attack of nerves, or a night's insomnia. Small dues. As for the fifty grand, he knew he could not have kept it anyway. It was not Jaeger's money. That swindler had got it from the many investors in his mutual-fund racket. The money would eventually get back to them. "Well," he said, "a small winner is better than a big loser. I got the five thousand retainer, and five thousand bucks ain't bubkas."

"Bubkas?"

"Beans."

"You got *me* out of it, Sam. Am I bubkas?"

"No, honey," said Sam. "Which reminds me." He took out his wallet and fished in it for yesterday's ticket on Sweetie Pie in the seventh at Belmont. The maître d' was just coming along with the screen, so Sam asked him if he happened to know the race results. He did not. "Ask Tom at the bar, will you? He always knows."

Alex went and came back with the information: Sweetie Pie at twenty to one.

Sam thanked him and gave him their order for lunch.

"And we have two more mint juleps in the freezer," Sam said. "We'll drink them while we're waiting."

"Right away, Mr. Kelly. Is the screen satisfactory, sir?"

"Perfectly."

When the maître d' had left, Sam gave the betting ticket to Devvy.

"For me, Sam? But it's worth two hundred dollars!"

"So? Is this the first time a gent ever gave you two hundred?"

Devvy looked hard at him. She was frowning. Her green eyes blazed. She took the betting ticket between thumbs and forefingers and slowly, delicately tore it to shreds. She dropped the shreds into the ash tray.

Then she leaned close to him and gently kissed him on the mouth.

"Silly boy!" she whispered. "Who needs two lousy hundred? I've got your five grand in my purse!"

# CHARTER BOOKS
## —the best in mystery and suspense!

# VICTOR CANNING

**"One of the world's six best thriller writers."**
— <u>Reader's Digest</u>

☐ **THE PYTHON PROJECT**　　　　69250-8　　　$1.95
A Rex Carver mystery. British and Russian agents have Rex on their open contract lists, but he's the only one who can untangle a scheme gone wrong.

☐ **THE DOOMSDAY CARRIER**　　　15865-X　　　$1.95
Rimster didn't have much time in which to find Charlie, a friendly chimp carrying a deadly plague bacillus. The problem was, he couldn't let anyone know he was looking!

☐ **THE KINGSFORD MARK**　　　　44600-0　　　$1.95
A novel of murder and betrayal "in the best Canning manner," with a fortune as the prize.

☐ **THE LIMBO LINE**　　　　　　　48354-2　　　$1.95
The Russians are kidnapping Soviet defectors and brainwashing them.

☐ **THE WHIP HAND**　　　　　　　88400-8　　　$2.25
A stunning espionage novel whose twists and turns end at Hitler's corpse.

☐ **DOUBLED IN DIAMONDS**　　　　16024-1　　　$2.25
Rex Carver returns in this brilliant novel of espionage and adventure.

☐ **THE RAINBIRD PATTERN**　　　　70393-3　　　$1.95
Someone had already staged two kidnappings and the victims could remember nothing. The third target is the Archbishop of Canterbury!

---

*Available wherever paperbacks are sold or use this coupon*

**C CHARTER BOOKS,** Book Mailing Service
P.O. Box 690, Rockville Centre, N.Y. 11571

Please send me the titles checked above. I enclose $_____.
Include 75¢ for postage and handling if one book is ordered; $1.00 if two to five are ordered. If six or more are ordered, postage is free.

NAME _____

ADDRESS _____

CITY _____ STATE _____ ZIP _____

Gc

# CHARTER BOOKS
## Suspense to Keep You On the Edge of Your Seat

---

**DECEIT AND DEADLY LIES**
**by Franklin Bandy**　　　　　06517-1　　　　**$2.25**
MacInnes and his Psychological Stress Evaluator could tell when anyone was lying, but could he discover the lies he was telling to himself?

**VITAL STATISTICS by Thomas Chastain　86530-5　$1.95**
A missing body, several murders and a fortune in diamonds lead J. T. Spanner through a mystery in which New York itself may be one of the suspects. By the author of *Pandora's Box* and *9-1-1*.

**THE KREMLIN CONSPIRACY**
**by Sean Flannery**　　　　　45500-X　　　　**$2.25**
Detente espionage set in Moscow as two top agents find themselves as pawns in a game being played against the backdrop of a Presidential visit to the Kremlin.

**THE BLACKSTOCK AFFAIR**
**by Franklin Bandy**　　　　　06650　　　　**$2.50**
A small town, a deadly medical mystery, and the corruption of power provide the dangerous mix in this new KEVIN MACINNES thriller.

**SIGMET ACTIVE by Thomas Page　76330-8　$2.25**
The author of the bestselling HESPHAESTUS PLAGUE presents another thriller proving it isn't nice to fool Mother Nature.

---

*Available wherever paperbacks are sold or use this coupon*

**CHARTER BOOKS,** Book Mailing Service
P.O. Box 690, Rockville Centre, N.Y. 11571

Please send me the titles checked above. I enclose $_____.
Include 75¢ for postage and handling if one book is ordered; $1.00 if two to five are ordered. If six or more are ordered, postage is free.

NAME _____

ADDRESS _____

CITY _____ STATE _____ ZIP _____

Xa

# Action And Adventure From The World Famous EDGAR RICE BURROUGHS

**The Efficiency Expert**          18900-8          **$1.95**
Jimmy Torrance has finally found himself a decent job, but members of Chicago's underworld would rather see him behind bars.

**The Girl From Farris's**          28903-7          **$1.95**
Once a "lady of the night," Maggie Lynch desperately wants to escape her past. When she does go "respectable" she discovers that there is always someone who remembers.

**The Deputy Sheriff of Commanche County**    14248-6   **$1.95**
Although all the evidence points to Buck Mason as the killer of Ole Gunderstrom, he knows he is innocent. Now all he has to do is prove it.

**The Bandit of Hell's Bend**          04746-7          **$1.95**
Another unforgettable Western adventure by one of the master storytellers of all time.

**The Girl From Hollywood**          28912-6          **$1.95**
The hard but satisfying life the Penningtons lead on their ranch is shattered when a Hollywood drug pusher appears on the scene.

**The Oakdale Affair**          60565-6          **$1.95**
Two bizarre and seemingly unconnected crimes in a small town are woven into a fantastic story which will keep you guessing right up to the surprising climax.

*Available wherever paperbacks are sold or use this coupon*

**CHARTER BOOKS**, Book Mailing Service
P.O. Box 690, Rockville Centre, N.Y. 11571

Please send me the titles checked above. I enclose $_____.
Include 75¢ for postage and handling if one book is ordered; $1.00 if two to five are ordered. If six or more are ordered, postage is free.

NAME _____

ADDRESS _____

CITY _____ STATE _____ ZIP _____

Ha

# CHARTER BOOKS

## Edgar Award Winner Donald E. Westlake
## King of the Caper

**WHO STOLE SASSI MANOON?**     88592-6     **$1.95**
Poor Sassi's been kidnapped at the film festival — and it's the most fun she's had in years.

**THE FUGITIVE PIGEON**     25800-X     **$1.95**
Charlie Poole had it made — until his Uncle's mob associates decided Charlie was a stool pigeon. See Charlie fly!

**GOD SAVE THE MARK**     29515-0     **$1.95**
Fred Fitch has just inherited a fortune — and attracted the attention of every con man in the city.

**THE SPY IN THE OINTMENT**     77860-7     **$1.95**
A comedy spy novel that will have you on the edge of your seat — and rolling in the aisles!

**KILLING TIME**     44390-7     **$1.95**
A small New York town: corruption, investigators, and Tim Smith, private investigator.

## The Mitch Tobin Mysteries
## by Tucker Coe

| | | |
|---|---|---|
| **THE WAX APPLE** | 87397-9 | **$1.95** |
| **A JADE IN ARIES** | 38075-1 | **$1.95** |
| **DON'T LIE TO ME** | 15835-8 | **$1.95** |

*Available wherever paperbacks are sold or use this coupon*

**CHARTER BOOKS,** Book Mailing Service
P.O. Box 690, Rockville Centre, N.Y. 11571

Please send me the titles checked above. I enclose $_____.
Include 75¢ for postage and handling if one book is ordered; $1.00 if two to five are ordered. If six or more are ordered, postage is free.

NAME _____

ADDRESS _____

CITY _____ STATE _____ ZIP _____

Ja

# CHARTER BOOKS
### Excitement, Adventure
### and Information
### in these latest Bestsellers

☐ **THE PROPOSAL**  68342-8  $2.50
A novel of erotic obsession by Henry Sutton, author of THE VOYEUR and THE EXHIBITIONIST.

☐ **CHESAPEAKE CAVALIER**  10345-6  $2.50
A passionate novel of early Colonial days, by Don Tracy.

☐ **BOOK OF SHADOWS**  07075-2  $2.50
A New York policeman, a beautiful actress, a coven of witches, and a Druid priest come together in this spine-tingling tale of horror.

☐ **THE ADVERSARY**  00430-X  $2.25
Out of the ashes of history a battle is brewing—a novel of occult power.

☐ **FIRE ON THE ICE**  23876-9  $2.25
Alaska is the setting for an explosive novel about the passions flying in our largest state.

Available wherever paperbacks are sold or use this coupon.

------------------------------------------------

**CHARTER BOOKS, Book Mailing Service
P.O. Box 690, Rockville Centre, N.Y. 11571**

Please send me the titles checked above. I enclose $_____.
Include 75¢ for postage and handling if one book is ordered; $1.00 if two to five are ordered. If six or more are ordered, postage is free.

NAME _____

ADDRESS _____

CITY _____ STATE _____ ZIP _____

Ka

# HEALTH AND BEAUTY—ADVICE FROM THE EXPERTS

☐ **COSMETICS: THE GREAT AMERICAN SKIN GAME**
30246-7  $2.25
The startling facts of the cosmetic industry are revealed by consumer advocate Toni Stabile.

---

☐ **LIVE LONGER NOW**  48515-4  $1.95
The bestselling book that details the Pritikin program of diet and exercise.

---

☐ **THE LIVING HEART**  48550  $2.95
The complete, illustrated book of the human heart, by Drs. DeBakey and Gotto.

---

☐ **LOW BLOOD SUGAR AND YOU**  49760-8  $2.25
Famed nutritionist Dr. Carlton Fredericks tells how to identify and treat this disease.

---

☐ **VITAMIN E: THE REJUVENATION VITAMIN**
71231-2  $1.95
How to obtain this vitamin for better health, longer life and greater sexual vigor.

---

☐ **HONEY FOR HEALTH**  34267-1  $1.50
Not only is honey a delicious energy source, it's a beauty aid and medicine, too.  Cecil Tonsley

Available wherever paperbacks are sold or use this coupon.

---

**C** **CHARTER BOOKS, Book Mailing Service**
**P.O. Box 690, Rockville Centre, N.Y. 11571**

Please send me the titles checked above. I enclose $_____.
Include 75¢ for postage and handling if one book is ordered; $1.00 if two to five are ordered. If six or more are ordered, postage is free.

NAME _____

ADDRESS _____

CITY_____ STATE_____ ZIP _____

# NICK CARTER

"America's #1 espionage agent."
—<u>Variety</u>

Don't miss a single high-tension novel in the Nick Carter Killmaster series!

☐ THE DAY OF THE DINGO   13935-3   $1.95
When a new agent turns up dead in Tokyo, Nick follows the trail of intrigue.

☐ AND NEXT THE KING   02277-4   $1.95
Nick's mission takes him to Spain where a bizarre assassination plot hinges on a night at the opera.

☐ TARANTULA STRIKE   79840-3   $1.95
KGB's top agent has been terminated — and Nick joins his beautiful replacement to find the assassin.

☐ STRIKE OF THE HAWK   79072-4   $1.95
Two special Nick adventures in one volume.

Available wherever paperbacks are sold or use this coupon.

---

**C** CHARTER BOOKS, Book Mailing Service
P.O. Box 690, Rockville Centre, N.Y. 11571

Please send me the titles checked above. I enclose $_____.
Include 75¢ for postage and handling if one book is ordered; $1.00 if two to five are ordered. If six or more are ordered, postage is free.

NAME _____

ADDRESS _____

CITY_____ STATE_____ ZIP _____

Ec